"I don't want you to get in trouble with Mrs. Shevvington," said Robbie quickly, looking around to be sure nobody heard. "You're new here, Christina. You don't know. *Don't speak up again like that.*"

"But you're new, too," protested Christina. "We're all new. We just started junior high. How can you know Mrs. Shevvington any better than I do?"

Robbie's eyes were old and dark. He said, "I have an older sister." He said no more, giving the sister no name, no description, as if his older sister truly were nothing more than that — not a person, not a soul — just a thing. Christina shivered. Robbie swallowed. Whispering, he added, "She — she had Mrs. Shevvington last year for senior English."

"And?" said Christina.

Robbie shrugged. He walked away. "Just don't talk back," he said over his shoulder.

His sister, then — had she talked back?

But what had happened to his sister?

Books in Caroline B. Cooney's
Point horror trilogy:

point

THE FOG

Caroline B. Cooney

SCHOLASTIC INC.
New York Toronto London Auckland Sydney

ISBN 0-590-43806-9

12 11 10 9 8 7   3 4 5/9

Printed in the U.S.A.   01

First Scholastic printing, August 1989

Chapter 1

It was very hot the last week before school began: as though the wind from another world were crossing the island.

Christina packed her trunks, filling them with the heavy sweaters and thick socks she would need for a Maine winter.

Her mother kept handing her things like long underwear and pajamas with feet. Hand knit mittens with snowflakes and bathrobes with hoods. Christina would never wear such things in front of mainland children. She put them on the bottom layer of the trunk, planning never to touch them.

Burning Fog Isle had only three hundred year-round residents. Twenty-eight miles out to sea, it was Maine's most famous, most beautiful island. And it had only four children between the ages of thirteen and seventeen, so once they finished sixth grade, they were sent to the mainland for junior and senior high.

Christina knew the town on shore almost as well

as the island; her father's truck and her mother's car were kept in garages by the dock; they went into town on Frankie's boat a couple of times a month; they saw movies and shopped, went to the dentist, and got sneakers on sale just like everybody else.

It was only school that Christina had not done like everybody else. Christina had never been in a school with classrooms, a cafeteria, hallways, bells that rang, art, music, gym, and hundreds of kids. Now she would be in junior high; instead of four friends, she would have dozens.

Christina had been told that going to the mainland would be an Advantage. "You will have Advantages there," people said.

Advantages sounded rather dull and sturdy, like winter socks.

Christina did not want any part of that. She wanted love, adventure, and wild, fierce emotions that would batter her, as storms battered the island. I am thirteen, Christina thought, I am ready. I want it all.

Christina finished packing. She and her mother lugged the trunk to the front hall and locked it. Christina put the key in her purse. She had never had a purse before. She had never needed one. Now she had her first key, her first handbag, her first allowance.

Christina hurtled over the pink-flecked granite that was the symbol of Burning Fog Isle — huge, diagonally thrusting cliffs sparkling with silver mica. She ran past strangled fir trees growing out of cracks and leaped over the pink rock roses that dusted the rims.

She found the other children gathered on the hill above the village. The heat had worn them down; they looked collapsed and sunburned.

Benjamin, who would be a sophomore, regarded school as a state-mandated prison between fishing seasons. He ached for his sixteenth birthday, when he could quit school. He would turn sixteen around Thanksgiving, and he planned to stop school right then, that afternoon, and go home on Frankie's boat. Benj was rightfully a lobsterman.

His brother Michael was going into ninth grade, and he had explained several times to Christina that ninth-graders never spoke to or associated with seventh-graders. She must not expect Michael to talk to her in school. If Christina tried to hold his hand, Michael would flatten her.

Michael was fourteen. Christina had adored him all her life, and Michael had not noticed it all his life.

Boys were always difficult.

But Anya? A beautiful, brilliant star of a student? Why was Anya not excited? It was going to be her senior year. Christina had always thought of senior year as a sort of heaven, glistening and full of rainbows.

But Anya was as tense and fidgety today as she had been all summer.

"It shouldn't be so hot," said Anya. "The ocean

like glass? The morning sky free of fog? Everything is wrong."

The children squinted in the glare of sun off the smooth water.

"You nervous about school starting, Christina?" asked Benjamin. Benj was never nervous. He was fifteen and solid. He had had his own lobster boat for years. Benj got up at four every morning, started the outboard motor like his father and uncle and cousins, and went out to sea.

Christina had read many books and Benj did not fit into any of them. He was the only fifteen-year-old boy Christina knew, but he had nothing in common with fifteen-year-olds in books. Benj was more like parents in books, only stronger. Nothing frightened Benjamin Jaye.

"Seventh grade isn't so bad." Benj said.

Christina did not know why he was asking if *she* was nervous. It was so clearly Anya who was. Anya shook her head, as if the strange stillness of the Atlantic Ocean bothered her ears.

Christina had always wanted to be and look just like Anya. Anya was very fair, and unlike everybody else on the island, whether year-around, day tripper, or tourist, Anya never tanned. Like a princess in a fairy tale, Anya remained chalk white, with a frame of black hair so thick and heavy it seemed to weight her slender neck.

"We get to stay at the Schooner Inne," said Christina to the older girl. "Aren't you excited about that?"

Schooner Inne was a lovely sea captain's house,

now a bed and breakfast, which usually closed down for the winter season. This year the Inne had new owners — the high school principal and his wife. They wanted to try staying open during winter and had agreed to take the four island children who had to board in town through the school year.

"It'll be luxury," Christina reminded Anya. She knew that Anya adored rich things.

Anya's parents were real Maine, and that meant they were poor. Anya hated being poor. She hated her tiny house, its shingles curled from the salt air, white trim peeling, enormous piles of lobster traps filling the little yard. Anya dreamed of cities: skyscrapers, escalators, high fashion, and taxis. She worked hard in school; striving, striving, striving to put Burning Fog Isle behind her and become somebody else.

Christina would be sharing a room at the sea captain's house with Anya. Christina was worried. What if she didn't please Anya? What if Anya grew angry with Christina for being younger, dumber, and duller? What if the town kids teased Anya for hanging around with a baby like Christina?

Mainland kids always teased island kids. Michael and Anya had given her instructions on how to handle the teasing. "Just laugh," they said. "No fists. It doesn't work. It gives the island a bad reputation."

Nobody was more "island" than Christina. Everybody who saw her called her "local color." She had had a thousand photographs taken of her, and been painted twice. "You are beautiful," the tourists and the artists would tell her, but they would ruin it by smiling slightly, as if it were a weird beauty or they were lying. She was as harsh and stern as the pink granite she stood on. This did not make Christina happy. She had never read anything in *Seventeen* about strength as beauty.

Christina was the only child she or the summer people had ever come across with tri-colored hair. Mostly dark brown, it was streaked with silver and gold. With every movement, Christina seemed to change color. She loved her hair and wore it just like Anya, but on Anya the mass of hair was magnificent, and on Christina it was a tangled thicket.

When Christina studied *Seventeen* magazine, analyzing models, make-overs, and teenage stars, she found no resemblance between herself and those girls — not hair, lips, eyes, cheekbones, posture — nothing.

If she did possess any beauty, Christina did not know what it consisted of.

The sea captain's house was beautiful. Symmetrical and graceful, high and white. Perhaps she would absorb some of that beauty just living there.

"The sea captain's wife," Anya said in a strange, glassy voice, "committed suicide."

"Oh, Anya," said Benj irritably. "That's just a legend, and anyway it was a hundred years ago and who cares?"

"It might have been weather like this when the sea captain's wife stepped off her roof," said Anya. She walked away from the other children to balance on a granite outcropping that rose from the Atlantic

Ocean like drowned rocks. She stared at the mirror of the sea as if reading her fortune in its seaweed-laden palm.

The sunshine poured out of the sky like liquid. The Atlantic did not move. Even though the tide was coming in, there was no sound of surf. No waves crashing against the rocks. No booming where air was slapped into rock pockets. The water just lay there, as if a personality stronger than the ocean itself had flattened it.

Below them, in the small, sheltered harbor of Burning Fog Isle, tourists gathered on the dock for the return boat to the mainland. Their baggage and suitcases littered the wharf. They crowded into the tiny souvenir shack, buying proof that they had visited the most famous island off the coast of Maine.

Christina thought, in a few days my island life will shut down. No longer one of the little children in the white schoolhouse, but off-island at last! Maybe I'll even have a boyfriend like Anya.

Anya's boyfriend was a very preppy townie named Blake. Blake had come out to the island once during the summer, as a surprise for Anya. Blake was dressed in what the children called Catalog Maine — a fine rugby shirt with wide stripes, high quality boat shoes without socks, and loose trousers made of imported cotton.

Christina was sure that what depressed Anya was not the strange weather, not the beginning of school, not having to room with somebody four years younger, and not even the oddity of boarding with the principal.

It was Blake. Her boyfriend had seen her as she really was — poor, island Maine. And would he, during their senior year, with SAT's, football season, college applications, prom, and graduation, still be interested in Anya Rothrock?

Frankie's boat nosed into the dock. The tourists jumped up and down with excitement. They got in the way, and their little children barely escaped falling into the water and getting crushed between boat and wharf. They abandoned the souvenir shack.

The souvenir shack was so dilapidated its roof had settled in a curve, and its door no longer closed. The shingles had fallen off the entire ocean side of the building. Winter weather would knock it down for good, and maybe the creature who ran it would never return.

The children called her a creature, rather than a woman.

She had skin like leather left out on the rocks — cracked and crusted. She wore fingernail polish as dark as dried blood, and several of her teeth were missing. She was the only person Christina had ever encountered who never went to the dentist.

The tourists clambered onto Frankie's boat. Frankie's dog, Rindge, snarled at all of them.

Frankie used to have a sweeter dog. Peg. How Christina had loved Peg! A soft Alaskan husky with eyes as blue as the sky. But Peg went overboard once to catch a hot dog a tourist tossed for her, and the sea was rough and Frankie couldn't get her back, even though she was a good swimmer.

Frankie tried so hard to reach Peg, and Peg tried even harder to swim back to him, but they didn't make it. Peg drowned.

Christina shivered, remembering.

She shook the memory away. "You know what we could get at the souvenir shop?" she said. "Posters for our bedroom walls! Let's all buy a poster."

Christina loved to imagine her room at the Schooner Inne. Would she have a bed with a lacy canopy? Wallpaper with sprigged flowers? Would there be a little desk beneath the window, so when she tired of doing homework, she could look out across the sea? She knew what she would have on her bed: the quilt her mother had made her. Each square on the quilt had a lovely name: falling star, bear's paw, flying geese. Dark reds, soft pinks, and rich blues tumbled together to make a work of art.

"I want a flower poster," announced Christina. "Manet or Monet, or whoever he is, or both."

But Anya did not want any posters in their room. "Let's not go down there," she said. "I'm afraid of that souvenir woman. Her eyes are too blue."

"I don't know where the souvenir woman spends the night," Christina told Anya.

"She doesn't sleep. Look at the hoods on those eyes. They aren't hinged for closing."

Anya whispered to Christina, "Those eyes are following me, Chrissie. Lobster eyes on stalks. Don't they remind you of Peg? That woman took Peg's dead eyes out of the ocean and stuck them in her own head."

Christina felt sick, almost dizzy. "That's the most

disgusting thing I ever heard, Anya," she said. "Don't talk like that." But the thought stayed with her: Peg, brown paws failing, slipping beneath the waves, only to have this creature seize her eyes. So that Peg swam on forever, without air, without sight.

The souvenir woman smiled, black holes where her teeth were missing, as if she had been shot. Slowly she pulled a poster out of the barrel. The woman moved toward the girls. Her layered skirts were long and thick, as leathery as her skin.

"If she touches me," said Anya, "I will turn to leather."

Christina swallowed. Already it seemed her throat had hardened, gotten thicker, turned leathery.

Anya stepped behind Christina, using her for a shield.

The souvenir woman rolled toward them, like a wave or a tire. The lobster eyes chose Anya. "I have a poster just for you." The poster in her claw-like hand was rolled picture side in, so it was only a plain white tube. "Come. Take it."

Christina shook her head. Anya laughed out of tune. "Don't let her touch me, Chrissie," whispered Anya.

Christina could think of nothing to say, either to the souvenir woman or to Anya. Would she be like this at school? Speechless and stupid in front of the sophisticated mainland kids?

"Yours," said the woman, with her dreadful smile.

"No, thank you," said Christina.

The woman laughed. Each eye focused separately; one eye for Anya, one eye for Christina. "No charge," said the woman to Anya. "I want you to have it."

Christina shook her head for both of them.

The woman jabbed Christina in the stomach with the poster, as if it were a lance or a sword. Behind her, Anya whimpered.

It's paper, Christina told herself, it's nothing but a piece of paper. I can just stuff it in the garbage as soon as I'm home.

She took the poster. In her hand it felt strangely damp, as if it were not made of paper at all, but of sea water.

"Come on, come on," Michael was saying, "don't take all day, Chrissie. Have you got the one you want?" He and Benj were each holding posters; they had somehow finished paying for them.

Christina stared down at the poster in her hand.

The souvenir woman smiled, blue eyes lying in her face like jellyfish dying on the rocks.

The children abandoned the village and went to Christina's house.

Burning Fog Isle had three kinds of houses: real ones, like Anya's or the boys; summer houses, built by vacationers; and summer cottages, built by millionaires generations ago.

To Christina the word "cottage" meant "castle." The cottage in which Christina and her family lived had thirty-two rooms. It had been built in 1905 by a family from Boston and was owned now by a family from Dallas who came up three weeks a summer, if they came at all.

Christina's family lived there year-round in the wing over the kitchens and pantries.

Christina's father could do anything: electricity, plumbing, carpentry, roof repair, gardening. It never bothered him that the Romneys didn't have a house of their own. He just slowly circled the cottage, year by year, painting and caulking his way around.

"What's your poster of?" Michael said to Christina.

"It's not my poster. I don't know what it's of," said Christina.

"You don't *know*?" said Michael. "What do you mean? You didn't look at it before you bought it? Christina, you are so strange."

Christina could not bear for Michael, whom she worshiped, to think her strange. "We didn't pick it out," said Christina. "She forced it on us."

"Who?" Michael asked.

"The woman who owns the shack," said Anya. "She made us take it."

"She was stabbing me with that poster," agreed Christina.

Michael was disgusted. "Christina, when you get to the mainland, you better not be yarning all the time. People don't make friends with people who yarn."

"I'm not yarning," protested Christina. "Weren't

you watching? Didn't you see her, all wrinkled and evil, forcing me to take this?"

"Don't use that word, *yarn*," said Michael. "It's island. It's local. You have to behave right once you're in school, Christina, or you'll get picked on. You say dumb things like 'wrinkled and evil' about some pitiful old woman who can't even afford to go to the dentist and you won't make any friends. You want to have friends, don't you?"

Christina could think of nothing more hideous than not having friends. The boys made it sound as if they would not be her friends either, should she go yarning around. Michael and Benj rolled their eyes. "And we have to live with her for a whole year," said Michael.

Christina flushed.

"Let's see this famous poster," said Benj.

Christina pulled the rubber band off the tube Anya took one corner of the poster and Christina the other, and together they held it open.

It was a poster of the sea.

The sea at its cruelest, the sea bringing destruction.

Green, blue, and black blended into a cauldron. Waves stretched up as if to rip a child off the rocks. White froth like beckoning fingers strangled little fish. Beneath the water blurry figures tried to swim up to the surface.

"Look," whispered Anya. Her long, thin fingers tightened convulsively on the paper. "You can see the drowned. Their bodies are floating at the bottom of the poster."

Christina found herself tipping forward, wanting to rescue everybody. It's paper, she reminded herself.

Anya stared into the poster. She swayed slightly, and her white skin grew even paler. "Look at the fingers of the dead," she whispered. "See them scrabbling at the surface?"

Michael inspected the poster. "Christina, you're so funny," he teased. "We live by the sea. It's eating the paint off our houses. It drowned our ancestors. Why do you want more of it? I can't believe you went and bought a poster of the sea."

Christina let go her corner. The poster folded up diagonally, so that a corner of sea stared from the long white tube.

"It drowned our ancestors," Anya repeated. "Perhaps it's been too long for the sea since it had a Romney. Or a Rothrock. Or a Jaye."

Christina rolled the poster sea side in and threw it in the grass. But then she picked it up again.

Chapter 2

There was shut-in fog the day they left: thick fog, like the inside of an envelope.

This was the fog for which the island was famous. A trick of atmosphere sometimes occurred, so that when the sun shone behind the fog, it looked like fire. Many times in the last three hundred years mainlanders had thought there was something burning at sea: a ship perhaps, in desperate need. But it had always been just the fog that hovered over the island.

Christina loved the fog. It hugged her and kept her secrets. It belonged to the sea and went back to the sea, and you could neither hold it nor summon it.

Anya hated fog. She insisted that her hair never looked good: She could work an hour setting her hair, walk out the door, and the fog would finger through her hair and ruin it.

The parents carried the children's trunks and boxes and suitcases on board Frankie's boat.

Dolly stood to one side and wept.

Dolly was Benj and Michael's little sister. She was also Christina's best friend. Only eight months younger than Christina, Dolly was in sixth grade, and, because they were the only girls anywhere near the same age, Christina and Dolly had always done everything together.

Dolly was small and wiry, with red hair in braids. "Christina gets to go to the mainland. Christina gets to go to real school. Christina gets to board at Schooner Inne. Have Anya for a roommate." Dolly ripped the top of her old white sneaker against the splinters of the dock. "Next year," said Dolly in grief, "when I get to board, Anya will have graduated. Benj will have quit school. It won't be the same! It's not fair. I want to go this year, too!" cried Dolly.

"Don't be silly," said her parents.

"Get lost," said her brothers.

Dolly had been born on Thanksgiving Day, and Mrs. Jaye let them use her for Baby Jesus in that year's Christmas pageant. She was only four weeks old and a ten-year-old Mary dropped Dolly headfirst into the manger, but there wasn't any brain damage, the doctor who was flown in told them. (Michael and Benj always said there was plenty, the worst kind.) Dolly wanted to be Baby Jesus every year. Dolly said it was pretty boring to have Jesus always either in diapers or dying on a cross, and why didn't we have a nice six-year-old Jesus (Dolly) or a really decent ten-year-old Jesus (Dolly), and now she said, "I'm almost as old as Christina, let me come to school, too!" But her parents hung onto her.

Christina was swept by panic. What if she didn't make friends? What if Dolly remained, forever, the only friend Christina ever had? What if Anya hated sharing a room with her and Michael and Benj hated sharing rooms with each other and everything was awful?

She hugged Dolly fiercely. Summer people laughed gently. Christina knew they thought of her as a pitiful little country girl who had never been off-island and was afraid of the Big Bad Mainland. Christina felt like spitting on them.

"Have a good time," whispered Dolly. "Send me tapes." She pressed into Christina's hand a beautifully wrapped present, which Christina knew, since they had mail-ordered it together, contained a half dozen new, blank cassette tapes on which Christina was to dictate all the news, tell Dolly every single detail, and on which, by return boat, Dolly would describe the island.

Frankie said, "Okay, now, we said our goodbyes? We sure? We absolutely done here? Huh, Lady Christina?" Frankie was very tall and thin; just skin tightened over lanky bones. He wore a Red Sox baseball cap and chewed a pipe. He never bought tobacco and never smoked; he just liked the pipe in his mouth.

"Done," said Christina, and she felt horribly, terrifyingly, "done" — as if she would never return to Burning Fog Isle. She said nothing, letting Dolly do all the weeping good-bye. She waved calmly to her parents and spoke in a relaxed fashion to Anya. The wind fingered their hair, making Anya's a dark storm and Christina's a mass of glowing ribbons. The tourists said how beautiful they were.

Frankie took the boat out into the solid gray of the ocean. They headed into the fog, and the island vanished; the fog soaked it up.

"The island has drowned," said Anya. She trailed her fingers in the fog. "Or have we drowned?"

One tourist murmured to his wife, "Don't those two girls look like ancient island princesses? Marked out for sacrifice?"

The wife did not laugh. "Sent away for the sake of the islanders," she whispered, "to be given to the sea."

Anya accidentally jogged Christina's arm.

The silvery-paper package with its pink and lavender ribbons was knocked out of Christina's hand. She tried to catch it, but it fell overboard. Frankie's boat surged on. The present floated in the waves, only the ribbons above water.

"It's an omen," said the summer people, laughing.

The children did not laugh.

"It's only tapes," said Christina, although she felt sick and desperate, because now how would she exchange with Dolly? She had not even read Dolly's good-bye card yet. Christina let herself cry a moment, knowing that her face was so damp from the fog nobody would be able to tell.

The boys had seen. They came out of the cabin to commiserate. Benj said not to worry; he would buy Christina another tape. I'm such a hick I forgot I could buy more, she thought. I forgot about stores.

Christina thought of her allowance. Her mother had given her five dollars a week. It sounded like a fortune, but Anya said it was nothing; Anya said Christina would be island poor and laughed at.

It was low tide when they docked. The pilings that held up the dock were long and naked, like telephone poles. They weren't pretty. They weren't symmetrically placed. They were just there.

Out in the harbor were friendship sloops, lobster smacks, visiting yachts, and cabin cruisers, trawlers, and Boston Whalers. The rich, sick, sea smell of bait was everywhere, coming from the herring in the barrels in the bait house.

Before them the town rose in layers.

There were the docks, boathouses, and fishmarkets. Then came the tourist lanes — boutiques; antique shops; boat, moped, and bike rentals; real estate agents, and ocean view inns. Next came the real town — gas station, bank, laundromat, shoe store, discount appliance store. Up on the hills were the houses, jammed next to each other. Layers of green tree and hill poked between roofs. Scarlet geraniums bloomed in dooryards.

The summer people clambered off Frankie's boat first, the way summer people always do. Michael and Benj began shouldering the trunks and boxes.

A wave of excitement as wild and strong as the ocean gales swept over Christina.

She was crossing a frontier.

Childhood jumped rope on the isle, but now she would put away childhood, and be a teenager. She would fend for herself and answer to none.

"Anya, I'm grown up now," she whispered, but Anya neither agreed nor disagreed. Anya's eyes were searching for the Shevvingtons.

The children were all old Maine stock, with old names. Benj, Michael, and Dolly were Jayes; Anya was a Rothrock; and Christina, a Romney. The sea captain's wife, who stepped off the roof all those generations ago, had been born a Rothrock like Anya. She had married Captain Shevvington.

The principal's name was Shevvington. Christina's father said that was why the school board hired him — to have a Shevvington back in town, to match Shevvington Street, Shevvington House Restaurant, and the Shevvington Collection in the Maritime Museum.

At orientation back in July, the island parents and children had met Mr. Shevvington. He had strange eyes. Unblinking and hypnotic, like a dog's. Christina had wanted to stare right back, but the mad dog image frightened her, as if to stare wrongly would make Mr. Shevvington bite her, and she would be mortally wounded and die in agony.

How impressed all the parents were with the principal! He's such a caring man! they said to each other. He's so understanding and yet so well disciplined. He's gentle with the children, but strong and firm. He will be a perfect role model for the boys and a father figure for the girls.

Christina had been amazed to hear her own parents talking like this, as if they had all just read the same pop psychology book.

Christina, Anya, and the boys stood on the dock, surrounded by piles of possessions. Trunks, cardboard boxes, tennis rackets, suitcases, tote bags, backpacks. Christina felt like an immigrant who would probably have to get shots before she would be allowed to stay.

High on the cliffs to their left, on the other side of the Singing Bridge, perched on top of Candle Cove, sat the Schooner Inne.

Nobody in his right mind would build on Candle Cove. It was a fine place for warehouses or factories, but not for homes.

Tide at Candle Cove was twenty-eight feet — as high as the roof of a house! The sides of the cove were rocks, huge outcroppings with ledges and shelves that appealed to children and romantics.

A hundred years before, a couple on their honeymoon had picnicked on a granite outcropping that was twenty-five feet above the mud. How happy they must have been, sharing lemonade, perhaps nibbling at the same scarlet apple. How exciting the tide must have seemed, rumbling forward, the waves leaping and lashing. And suddenly the two lovers must have realized that twenty-five feet was not high enough to be safe from a twenty-eight foot tide. Christina imagined them trying to get off the ledge, the boy lifting the girl, her long skirts snagging, the water roaring around them, the boy thinking *No, no, no, no, please don't* —

Their bodies were never found. The sea took them to picnic forever and ever. The town had fenced off the cliff around Candle Cove, but still people went down there, climbing on the rocks, or worse, walking on the mud flats exposed at low tide.

If nobody in his right mind would build on Candle Cove, thought Christina, then the sea captain was not in his right mind when he built his house. Why did his bride step off the roof?

"If the Shevvingtons don't hurry up and get here," said Benj irritably, "we'll use your father's truck to haul this stuff to the Inne, Christina. You got keys?"

"Of course she doesn't have keys," said his brother. "She's only thirteen. She doesn't know how to drive."

A solid trunk of a woman appeared between them. She had no female shape at all. She was without curves: a large thick post with hair on top. Even her head had no curves. Her features were very flat, so that she had no profile, only a face. "There will be no bickering in my household," she said, laying a hand on the shoulders of the brothers. Her hands were fat, the flesh bulging over the many rings on her short fingers. The nails were long and hooked and had just been polished dark red, so that they seemed to bleed.

Michael and Benj, who, with their sister Dolly, had never done anything except bicker, pulled away from her hands.

"I am Mrs. Shevvington. Load your belongings into the van. Do not dillydally. There will be no dillydallying in my household."

Christina could not imagine this pie dough wed to Mr. Shevvington. Many years and many pounds separated them. Mr. Shevvington was so graceful, handsome, and silvery.

The creature closed her thick, curved palm over Christina's cheek. "Dillydallying?"

"No, no," said Christina, leaping away from the hand. It was sweaty. It had left a damp print on her cheek.

The boys began loading the mountain of possessions into a dark green utility van with rust along the bottom. A driver sat motionless behind the steering wheel.

Mrs. Shevvington commented that they had brought a considerable amount with them; she did not know where they thought they would store all these things. Certainly she, Mrs. Shevvington, did not propose to have her precious space given up to old tattered suitcases.

"You have an inn," protested Christina. "You must be able to store a million suitcases and trunks."

"When I state a fact, Christina, do not contradict me."

Christina flushed. The others looked embarrassed for her.

Their posters had been rolled into one cardboard shipping tube, which had fallen on the dock. "Is this garbage?" Mrs. Shevvington asked.

"No, I just didn't see it," said Benj.

"Sloppy," said Mrs. Shevvington. "There will be no sloppy thinking or acting in my household."

Benjamin's smile faltered and vanished. Christina's face would not even form a smile. She has flattened all our faces to match hers, thought Christina, and we have known her only for a minute.

Mrs. Shevvington waved the van away. It drove off without them.

"We will walk," said Mrs. Shevvington. "It is a brisk walk, straight up Breakneck Hill. Good for you."

Michael nodded. "There will be no laziness in your household, huh, Mrs. Shevvington?" he said, with his most charming smile, the smile that won all the summer visitors over and made them come back the next year.

Mrs. Shevvington smiled. Her teeth were as short as her fingernails: tiny yellowed stubs that hardly seemed like teeth at all. Michael's sweet smile vanished slowly, as if being erased. When Michael's smile was entirely gone, Mrs. Shevvington closed her own lips. Her face remained solid. "It is called Breakneck Hill," she said, "because a hundred years ago, when bicycles first came into fashion, a young boy — about your age, Christina — rode his bicycle down that hill. Of course it was too steep for the rudimentary brake his cycle possessed."

"What happened to him?" Michael asked.

Mrs. Shevvington raised thin wispy eyebrows. "He broke his neck, of course."

I don't want to live with her for a year, Christina thought. I can't bear to sit at breakfast with her, or sort laundry with her, or have her say good night.

Christina wanted to run back down Breakneck Hill and leap back on the boat with Frankie, where

24

Rindge would wag his tail and keep her safe, with his salty, doggy smell.

How could the others walk so calmly up Breakneck Hill?

Christina looked back. Frankie was already leaving. She clung to the safety fence, and it wobbled beneath her grip.

Breakneck Hill was very steep, and no effort had been made to terrace it. It hurt their feet to walk at such a tilt. The wind tore at them, alternately pushing them away from the edge and yanking them toward it. In winter, spray from the waves would glaze the sidewalk with ice.

It must have been a tragic time, a hundred years ago, she thought, what with the boy on the bike, the honeymooners, and the sea captain's wife.

Mrs. Shevvington handed Anya the poster tube to carry, and Anya went white and shivered, taking it.

Michael pointed down into the mud flats that spread on either side of the channel. Out on the flats walked a man in a wet suit. The wet suit was brown rather than the usual black, and it was hard to distinguish the man from the mud. He seemed bodyless. Skinless. Rubbery and slick.

"Idiot," said Mrs. Shevvington. She sounded rather pleased, as if she liked comparing herself favorably to idiots. She paused to watch the man.

They were directly over Candle Cove, with breathtaking views out to sea and into Maine.

The tide crept slowly in. Licking the barnacles,

inching toward the docks and the town, it slithered along like a great flat fish.

The man in the brown wet suit looked at the pancake of water and cocked his head, as if wondering whether to bother about it.

A queer, sickening whisper had begun.

Benj said, "It's the tide. It's coming." He ran to the edge of the cliff and leaned over the flimsy wire. "Get out!" he yelled at the wet suit. "Get out of the cove! Now!"

Christina, whose life was governed by tides, had never seen a tide like this. Although she had sat on the town docks a hundred times as this very tide came in, and from safety had laughed at its power, she had never seen the tide from above — the horror of the ocean coming home to Candle Cove.

The pancake of flat water that had crawled over the mud flats rippled, as if monsters were writhing in it.

The wet suit began running now, in a horrible slow pattern, like a man living out all Christina's nightmares: his feet caught, the mud sucking on him.

The wet suit reached one of the ladders that stuck down into the cove like trellises for roses.

The water at his feet buckled like a milkshake in a blender.

The wet suit ran up the ladder, and the water ran with him, eating his ankles.

The rest of the ocean hurtled into the narrow granite opening of the Cove. It was loud as thunder, loud as a rock concert when you're sitting next to the stage.

Tons of green water crashed toward the docks.

As the first wave passed beneath them, the children actually tasted it. The wind lifted salt up toward them, and the air was colder from the cold of the Atlantic, and it brushed their cheeks with ocean air.

Anya cried out, but her cry was drowned by the crash of the tide.

The wet suit made it.

He stood only inches above the waves that had tried to taste him, and delicately shook off his feet to get rid of clinging seaweed.

The wet suit did not seem like a person, but like brown rubber that moved. Christina wanted to say so but she was afraid to yarn in front of Mrs. Shevvington. When she looked around for comfort, Mrs. Shevvington's one-dimensional face horrified Christina as much as the wet suit.

Christina took Anya's arm for support.

Anya was smiling insanely. It was a weird, glowing smile, as if something fluorescent moved inside her. "You don't want to be here this year after all, do you?" whispered Anya. "For all your dreams of freedom, and first love, and sea captains' houses, you know it's wrong, don't you, Christina? The sea is wrong, the year is wrong, the — "

"Anya," said Benj, "stop making Chrissie nervous. She's got enough to worry about, starting junior high."

Chapter 3

The sea captain had built his house solidly — white
clapboard with shutters in a green so dark it was
almost black, like the sea in bad weather. There
was no land around the Inne: The back steps opened
onto the sea cliffs, and the front steps opened right
to the street. Stapled to the cliff edge, high above
the sea, the house loomed against an empty sky as
if there were not one thing between the house and
Europe.

Mrs. Shevvington slid her key into the gleaming
brass handle of a green front door so large three
people could walk in at once. The door swung silently open.

Inside, the hall was narrow, with narrow stairs
going steeply up, as if the captain had forgotten this
was a mansion he was building, not a crowded ship.

Christina looked up the stairwell. It was like
looking up a lighthouse. The steps ran in ovals, curv-
ing at the landings. High, high above, the glass in
the cupola glittered in the September sun. The cupola did not seem to have a floor. Christina was

disappointed. "I thought you could sit up there," she said to Mrs. Shevvington. She had thought of herself with a book, binoculars, and a bag of potato chips, sitting tucked away in the cupola, with the best view in Maine all to herself.

"No. It is unsafe. It can be reached only by a ladder. Never go up there." Mrs. Shevvington made it sound as dangerous as picnicking on railroad tracks. "If I find I cannot trust you children to stay away from it," said Mrs. Shevvington, her voice slowing down and getting rougher, "I will have to take Steps."

In the dining room, black-and-gold willow trees arched over narrow bridges, while black peacocks strutted in stone-littered gardens. What strange wallpaper, thought Christina.

"The sea captain sailed to Japan a lot," said Mrs. Shevvington in explanation. "House has the original wallpaper. Very historic. Nothing children should ever be near," she added, glaring, as if they were already attacking the walls with crayons.

"Are there any guests right now?" Christina asked.

"No."

Michael started to walk into the dining room but Mrs. Shevvington caught his shoulder. What strength was in that grip. Michael froze like a child playing Stone Tag. His mobile face and laughing mouth became solid, his knees stiff; he was a tilted statue.

"These rooms are not for you," said Mrs. Shevvington. "These rooms are for paying guests." She let go of the statue and he turned back into Michael.

"We pay," Christina objected.

"A pittance from the town; it's hardly an income."

Michael rubbed his shoulder where her hand had been attached.

"And do not run down the stairs. It will bother the guests, and you might fall."

It was Christina's opinion that there was no way to get down a staircase except by running. And she had never fallen in her life.

Mrs. Shevvington showed them the formal living room. It too was Oriental in flavor, with shiny lacquered furniture and pearl inlaid flowers.

Christina was beginning to have sympathy for the bride who had hurled herself off the cliff. Who could be comfortable in rooms full of black-and-gold peacocks?

"For guests," said Mrs. Shevvington.

She showed them a library. Walls of shelves, but very few books. Big leather chairs and a bare desk.

"For guests," said Mrs. Shevvington.

"But we're guests, too," Christina said.

Mrs. Shevvington led them into the kitchen, which was enormous. It must have been remodeled in the 1950s, because it had rows of white metal cabinets with curved edges. The countertops were green marbleized Formica with stainless steel rims. Near the sink tiny steel cabinets with little doors opened to reveal rolls of waxed paper and aluminum foil, waiting to be torn off. A very large table with a white surface and wooden legs as thick as thighs sat in the middle of the room.

Christina thought it was the ugliest kitchen she had ever seen in her life.

The Atlantic Ocean pounded outside. But even when Christina stood at the sink and drew up on her tiptoes to look out, she could not see the water.

Off the kitchen was a small, dark room, filled with old sagging furniture, the kind people left in beach houses rented out by the week. It had a small black-and-white television and a worn stack of last year's magazines. "You children will be using this room," said Mrs. Shevvington.

Christina waited for the others to object. She had spoken up several times; it was their turn — they were older.

But Anya merely stood with the poster of the sea in her hand as if she were glued to it. Michael was staring at his shoelaces. Benj was playing with his Swiss army knife.

Well, all right, if they wanted to be toads and get run over by a truck like Mrs. Shevvington, they could stay silent. Christina had never made a habit of staying silent. She had yelled at summer residents who dropped soda cans on the rocks and summer artists who abandoned paint tubes among the wildflowers. She had yelled at summer yachters who had the nerve to tie up at her father's slip, so that when he came into the harbor he had no place for his own boat on his own island.

Christina was more than capable of yelling at anyone.

She turned to yell at Mrs. Shevvington.

Mrs. Shevvington's eyes moved inside her flat

head. The eyes seemed to separate from her face, like movable eyes in an oil painting. "Yes, Christina?" she said very softly. She inclined her head toward Christina, like a guillotine in slow motion.

Christina looked at Michael and Benj and Anya for support. Surely this was not how mainland people normally treated island boarders.

Mrs. Shevvington smiled at Christina. Her horrid little teeth were like kernels of corn on a shriveled ear.

The poster of the sea fell out of Anya's hand.

"Our parents — " Christina began, leaning over to pick up the poster. But she got no further.

Mr. Shevvington entered the room.

Christina recognized him from the orientation of the previous July. How handsome he was! What fine features he had — not squashed and rubbery like his wife's, but sharp and defined. He wore a suit, which to Christina was very unusual. Nobody on the island ever wore one. The suit was soft gray, with the narrowest, most subtle pinstripes and in the breast pocket a dramatic red paisley silk handkerchief. Christina longed to touch the handkerchief. It was city fabric, city style.

She saw her parents suddenly as hicks, who would never own any handkerchief except Kleenex.

Christina looked into Mr. Shevvington's eyes. They were soft and gray, as welcome as spring rain.

"Children. What a pleasure. We've been getting ready for you all summer." With his fist he tilted Christina's chin up and kissed her forehead. She felt that if she were to ask for the silk hanky he would give it to her, that he would give her anything, and therefore she could not bear to ask him for a single thing. His height was perfect, the way he loomed over her was protection, his shadow was warmth.

"Christina," he said, "we don't want to worry our parents, now, do we? There are going to be adjustments we'll all have to make, learning how to live under one roof and get along."

He said he knew he could trust Christina never to be difficult or cause scenes. He said a child who loved her parents would write only cheerful letters, make only happy phone calls, because love meant never worrying your mother and father.

His smile moved across all four of the children, binding them, requiring smiles in return, like signatures on a contract, so they could never forget, never be bad. They would always adjust.

He said, "Christina, I can see already that you're going to be the spokeswoman of the group. I'm very impressed. A girl of your age, and already so articulate."

She felt as warm as if she had been toasting in front of a fire. Christina resolved never to tell her parents if she had any problems. A girl who was in junior high was old enough to take care of herself and protect her parents from worry.

Mr. Shevvington laughed and turned to his wife. "Candy, we're going to enjoy Christina, aren't we?" he said.

Candy? Her name is Candy? Christina thought. Impossible.

"Anya," Mr. Shevvington said now. He kissed

her in just the same way, fist under Anya's delicate chin, his lips planted on her forehead. "You are looking as beautiful as last year. We expect great things of you during your senior year, Anya." He surveyed her with the attention of a student learning the details of a piece of art.

Anya smiled up into Mr. Shevvington's eyes. "I won't let you down," she said, her voice full of emotion. "I'll do anything you say."

The principal smiled. It was a flat, bright smile, like the glassy sea on the day they got the posters. "I know," he said.

The Shevvingtons are sticky, Christina thought. Like the back of a stamp. I'm afraid of them.

Mrs. Shevvington's arm went around Christina's shoulder, and it tightened in what might have been a hug, or the first move of a strangle.

The principal spoke to Benj, saying he knew this school year was going to be so wonderful that Benj would never want to quit. Benj looked bored, but he didn't bother to argue, and just nodded.

Mr. Shevvington shook hands with Michael, saying that as a ninth-grader Michael was eligible for Junior Varsity and, with Michael on the teams, the school would have a splendid athletic year.

Anya turned her face toward the principal like a sunflower to the sky.

"I'm sorry I can't have lunch with you," Mr. Shevvington said, his handsome features drooping with distress. Anya's face mirrored his. "But I must run back to the high school to deal with some annoying odds and ends before we open in the morning." His face re-lit. "First day of class! You kids pretty excited?"

The boys remained bored.

Anya nodded joyfully. A puppy in a litter, thought Christina, wagging a tail for him.

"Upstairs," said Mrs. Shevvington, steering them through the halls. Christina was slow to obey. Mrs. Shevvington pushed her. It was like being touched by a jellyfish. Flesh soft and flaccid, as if there were no bones beneath the white surface.

The Jaye brothers were already racing upstairs. "Third floor," said Mrs. Shevvington. "Mr. Shevvington and I and the guests are on the second floor."

The boys' feet pounded on thick vermilion carpet up to the second floor and then sounded completely different — heavier, drummier.

There's no carpet on our stairs, thought Christina, and it seemed a metaphor for the year to come — there would be no carpet on this year.

"Your rooms are a bit bare," Mrs. Shevvington said. "But you may decorate any way you wish." She stayed at the bottom while the children circled the long, climbing stairs.

At the second floor a white-banistered balcony ran all the way around the open stairs, and numbered doors opened off it. One door was open. Inside, a white nubbly rug lay beside a shiny brass bed, and a puffy pink comforter matched balloon curtains. A delicate nightstand, white with gold trim, held a tiny hobnail glass lamp and a pretty little antique clock.

Let my room be like that! Christina thought.

The gentle curve of the stairs became tighter. The carpet stopped. The stairs were plain wood, and scuffing feet had worn hollows in the treads. The banisters needed dusting; the little knobs and whorls of the posts were black with grime.

The room that Anya and Christina were to share was at the top of the stairs. The door opened right onto the stairs. Christina thought, If we miss the bathroom at night, we'll fall all the way. Break every bone until we hit bottom.

Anya and Christina's room had a bare wood floor, white walls, no curtains, just paper shades yellow with age. Twin beds without headboards wore plain white sheets and old mustard-colored blankets tucked in hard, like a punishment. Unmatched chests of drawers stood next to each other. Under the eaves, two closets were lit by bare bulbs on pull strings.

Christina wanted to cry.

Anya took a deep breath. "Better than where I stayed before," she said, sliding her trunk with her knee toward the further bed.

"*Better?*" said Christina, shocked.

"I didn't tell you on the island, because you'd have told your parents and worried them. They don't like us here. The people in this town. They're against us. You'll see. That's why we're living with the Shevvingtons. Mr. Shevvington is so kind! He's so thoughtful. He knew how hard it was for Michael and Benj and me last year, separated, living in ugly places with mean people because nobody else would take us. Mr. Shevvington is the only one on our side, Christina. He's all we have."

"Side?" Christina repeated.

"It's them against us," Anya said. Anya chose a chest of drawers. She opened her trunk and took out lilac-scented, flowered liner paper for the drawers. Anya was so well organized she had packed her scissors right next to it, and calmly she began cutting lengths of paper and laying them in her drawers. A faint scent of lilac filled the room.

Christina could not bear to start unpacking in this gloomy attic. She crossed the balcony to check out the boys' room. It too was bare as bones. But the boys had had no dreams of lace and satin. They flung their stuff around, bounced on the beds, and seemed pleased. The boys' walls were the same blackish green as the outside shutters. "My Marilyn Monroe poster will look really great up here," Michael said to Christina. Then he shouted down the stairwell, "Can we scotch tape things right to the walls, Mrs. Shevvington?"

"Of course not," muttered Christina. "In a house where you can't run down the stairs and can't enter the living room and can't eat in the dining room, you think you're going to be allowed to put scotch tape on walls?"

Christina leaned over the balcony rail. Mrs. Shevvington was standing at the bottom. "Certainly," she called.

Christina went back into their bedroom.

"Here," said Anya. "I cut you drawer liners, too." Christina had never lined a drawer in her life. At least there was one pretty thing in here. Too bad it had to lie hidden by her clothing.

A single window filled the only dormer, making a tiny alcove. Far below, the surf boomed, and the spray tossed. Christina examined the view, down Breakneck Hill, over the rooftops, and beyond to the hills. She picked out the garage where her father's truck and her mother's car were locked up. "Where did you board last year, Anya?"

Anya squeezed into the dormer beside Christina. After a moment of searching she pointed to an ugly, squat building the color of fungus.

Christina shivered. "How could you stand it? Why didn't you say how awful it was?"

Anya shrugged. "I don't exactly live in a magnificent beach house myself, remember. And even if things are bad, you can't tell anybody. It just worries people back on the island. They can't do anything about it anyway."

Christina's parents had always been able to solve anything. But they were islanders, and still on the island. They did not wear silk paisley handkerchiefs in their suit pockets. Anya was right. Looking at the strength of the sea made Christina strong. She remembered she was granite. She thought, What's the big deal? We can make the room pretty. And I'll never tell the others that the Shevvingtons make me nervous, because that's yarning, and they won't be friends with me if I yarn.

Them against us. What did that mean? Did it mean — could it possibly mean — that Christina would have no friends in seventh grade — no allies but Michael and Benj and Anya — no one on her side but Mr. Shevvington?

The tide continued to rise rather gently, considering its first cannonade.

"It really sounds like somebody puffing out birthday candles, doesn't it?" Anya said. She pushed the window open. The two girls crammed themselves through the opening and leaned into the salty air. The window was tall for so small a dormer. The windowsill pressed just above Christina's knees. *If somebody wanted to shove us out the window . . . ,* Christina thought.

She suddenly wondered where the poster of the sea was. The center of her back crawled, and Christina tried to turn in the small space, thinking —

Anya grabbed her. "Look!"

It was the man (woman?) in the wet suit. Still there. Still standing on the opposite cliff of Candle Cove.

He — it — waved at the girls.

Anya waved back.

Christina could not bring herself to make a human communication with a creature so lacking in human features. It was like Mrs. Shevvington, rubbery and flattened.

Anya jerked back into the room, yanking Christina with her, knocking both their skulls against the window frame. "What's the matter?" Christina asked. Her head hurt. She rubbed the dent.

Anya's white finger trembled, pointing. "There's your present from Dolly," she whispered.

It was borne in on the next wave, riding neatly on top, its metallic bow still gleaming.

"The ocean knows where you are," Anya said. She laughed madly. "It followed us here."

Mrs. Shevvington called them down for lunch.

They ate in the kitchen.

Christina had been hoping for peanut butter and jelly sandwiches, chicken noodle soup, and potato chips, which was her idea of the perfect noon meal. Mrs. Shevvington had made red flannel hash with poached eggs laid on top of each helping.

Christina did not know what to do. She loathed soft eggs, and the sick horrid way the yellow spurted around, like blood. She hated onions, and she especially hated beets. As for leftover corned beef, it should be fed to the sea gulls, not gagged down by human beings. "Mrs. Shevvington," said Christina as courteously as she knew how, "may I make myself a sandwich instead?"

Mrs. Shevvington looked truly shocked, as if Christina had done something quite rude and socially unacceptable. "Christina, common courtesy requires you to eat what is put before you."

Christina flushed.

Michael and Benj, who were of the shovel school of eating, had already begun shoveling. Michael used the side of his fork to cut his helping into squares, which he put into his mouth as if he were laying tiles. Yellow egg yolk dripped off his fork.

Mrs. Shevvington smiled.

Christina swallowed to stop herself from gagging. She drank her milk.

It was whole milk. Christina hated whole milk; it was thick and disgusting. She drank only skim, which was like blue water, and thirst quenching. Her fingers tightened around the glass.

She said to herself, We are paying to be here. We are guests. Just like any other guests. And I hate egg yolks. I'll throw up. She said, "Mrs. Shevvington, I'm sorry, and if we were going to be visiting for one night, I would eat anything with a smile, but we're going to be here for a year. So we should get straight what we can and can't eat."

Mrs. Shevvington's eyes lay in her head like the poached eggs on the hash. Rounded and glossy and soft.

"I don't like corned beef and poached eggs," said Christina.

"Christina, one reason you are here is to learn civilized behavior, get along with other people."

"But I get along fine with other people," Christina said. "The tourists are always taking my photograph, and — "

"Christina! Boasting is the quickest way to make enemies. I hope you realize that island children, especially island girls, have a hard time getting along. You must try much harder than this, Christina. Your task is to make the island proud of you, not ashamed."

Michael and Benj and Anya did not speak up. Was she really being horribly rude? Would Anya scream at her tonight, in that soft hissing rage she could drum up, saying, "Christina, what is the matter with you? Why can't you behave?"

"Eat your eggs, Christina," Mrs. Shevvington said. "In this house you eat what is put before you or go hungry."

Christina looked at the yellow blood running over her plate. She set her fork back down on her napkin, linking her fingers together in her lap like chains. She felt as if they had just declared war, she and the principal's wife.

Christina was so hungry. Breakfast at home had been a long time before and a long sea trip away. What was so terrible about making a sandwich?

Nobody talked. They ate seriously, as if it were a chore.

Christina's mother never allowed silence, either at home or at her restaurant at mealtimes. If nobody talked Mrs. Romney interrogated them and made them contribute. I don't actually want to be at war with her, thought Christina. How can I come home to runny yellow eggs every night? So I shall make friends. "Is running the Inne your full-time job, Mrs. Shevvington?" she asked politely.

A tiny yellow smile curled on her pie dough face. "No," said Mrs. Shevvington. "This isn't my only job. I am also the seventh-grade English teacher, Christina."

They spent the afternoon unpacking. Anya hummed as she stacked neat little piles of bikini panties and lacy bras. Christina hated being neat.

It took so much effort and who cared? But obviously Anya cared, and they had to learn to live together. This was what being roommates was — stacking your panties if the other person stacked hers.

Christina finished first because she had fewer clothes, no accessories, and, according to Anya, lower standards of neatness. She sat cross-legged on her bed watching Anya. Anya finished. She too sat on her bed. But she rocked backwards, as if something were tipping her. "Christina, when did you put it up?" whispered Anya. "I thought — I thought you were going to throw it out."

The poster of the sea was fastened to the wall over Christina's bed.

"I didn't touch it," Christina said. She turned to look, but her neck felt stiff, it was hard to turn all the way. "Hey, Michael!" she yelled. "Benj! You come in here and put our poster up?"

"Why would we go in your room?" Michael yelled back.

Anya put her hands over her ears. "They're talking to me," she whispered, her eyes darting around like minnows. "I can hear them. Chrissie, can you hear them?"

The boys have the only roll of tape, Christina thought. They must have come in here to put it up. "Somebody put it up," she said irritably.

"Chrissie," whispered Anya, "it's wet in here."

Christina stared at her roommate. Anya's thin graceful hands were arched toward the ceiling like a ballerina stretching toward the sky.

"They're calling to me," Anya whispered. Her

breath came in spurts; she was panting. "Can you hear them, Chrissie?"

"No," Christina said. "Anya, hold my hand."

"I don't want to swim," Anya cried. "I hate the water, I hate boats, I hate the island." Her hands weren't graceful, they were frantic — pumping — reaching — struggling. "Pull me out, Chrissie, they're touching me, I can feel their fingers, they almost have me — they — "

Christina grabbed one of the wild arms. Anya stared past Christina's face, her eyes huge. "The fingers," she cried.

What fingers? Christina thought. She did not let go of Anya. Christina smelled mothballs as her face pressed into the blanket.

"All right!" Michael shouted. "Action!" The boys thudded into the room, jumped on top of Christina and Anya, and began wrestling, throwing pillows and lashing towels. Michael's towel flicked with loud snaps against walls and skin. Christina grabbed the end of his towel and jerked him to the floor, where Anya, giggling, rolled him under the bed. Benj bounced on the bed like a trampoline. They were shouting and laughing when Mrs. Shevvington's voice cut like a chain saw, buzzing and cruel.

"There will be no roughhousing here. There will be no fighting. You boys stay out of the girls' room, do you hear me? There will be decent behavior at all times. Christina, did you start this?"

Night fell.

Christina's first night away from her parents, her

first night at Schooner Inne, her first night with a roommate.

Outside, the town ceased to move. It slept, cars silent, lights off.

There was no sound on the earth but the sound of the sea.

Long after midnight they were still awake.

They learned why nobody had built houses on Candle Cove — nobody but the sea captain, whose wife threw herself to her death among the tons of green water that leaped up to meet her.

Noise.

The children had grown up with the battering drum of surf and storm; their island had inured them to all sounds of the sea.

Or so they had thought.

Every six hours and thirteen minutes, there is a tide: Two low and two high tides occur every twenty-four hours and fifty-two minutes.

Tide began at one A.M. with an eerie slushing sound, like tires caught in snow. It woke all four of them up — Michael and Benj in their room by the road, and Anya and Christina over the Cove.

The slushy sound became louder, like violins tuning up. Michael and Benj came into the girls' room. They sat on Christina's bed under the poster. Like engines revving for the Indianapolis 500, the fury of the tide increased. Like rockets, the sea burst in, attacking the harbor in a tidal wave of fury, hitting the cliff below Schooner Inne with a slap so great it blocked their minds to anything but sound. The sounds did not stay outside, but came into the room; they were swimming in noise.

In fifteen minutes it was over.

The waves were just the waves.

"How do we sleep through that?" Christina said. "And it will be different every night. Tomorrow it'll start at one-thirteen, and the night after that at one twenty-six."

Outside the window the ocean chuckled and slithered.

"Listen," whispered Anya.

They listened.

Anya stood in the moonlight, a long thin white nightgown draping her slender body, her hair ruffling like dark ribbons in the night wind. "The sea can smack the rocks like a hand smacking a cheek. It can hiss or gurgle or even kiss. But when it wants, it can go quiet. And then," said Anya Rothrock, "you can hear the voices of the drowned."

The waves had settled into an irregular rhythm of rolls and crashes.

"The sea keeps count," Anya whispered. "The sea is a mathematician. The sea wants one of us."

Chapter 4

They woke early.

Morning light poured through the eastern windows.

The sun lay scarlet-and-gold on the horizon like a jewel on pale blue velvet.

The temperature had dropped sharply. It was Maine again. Chilly and windy.

Christina got out of bed shivering, and went to the window. It was low tide. The rich smell of the sea rose to greet her. Far out in the water the motors of lobster boats buzzed. She could not see as far as Burning Fog, and it was not one of the mornings in which the fog burned. Only bright, tossing waves quivered against the sky.

On a rock not quite large enough to be called an island, cormorants were spreading their wings to dry. These birds soaked up water when they dove for fish, and, eventually, as they paddled, sank so low in the water they were in danger of drowning. Then they had to mount a rock and hold up their wings for the wind to blow them dry. Christina had always thought it must be a very tiring way to live.

Anya rolled over and over until she had mummified herself in the sheets. "I hate getting up," she informed Christina. "Someday my life is going to begin mid-afternoon instead of dawn."

Christina just smiled. She loved mornings. The sun rose as early on Burning Fog Isle as any other place in the United States. In her bedroom back home, she liked to think she was the first American to see the sun coming over the horizon.

Anya sat up slowly, arching like a gymnast, hair draping her back. She yawned and stretched. Goose bumps rose on her thin, white arms. "Oh, no," she wailed. "It's cold out! Now the clothes we picked are no good. They were for hot weather."

The girls scrambled through their drawers, holding up sweaters, pants, and blouses, as if the correct choice would make or break the entire school year.

Christina settled for brand new jeans, a soft yellow shirt, and a cotton sweater with darker yellow cables. She tugged at the collar until she was satisfied with the way it poked up. So schoolgirl, she thought. She looked enviously at Anya, whose silver necklace and earrings glittered against the soft folds of her navy blue shirt.

Christina loved the way Anya's white throat showed where the blouse opened, and how the silver rope lay carelessly, and how Anya's cloud of black hair flowed over the clothing. Christina had never owned any jewelry to speak of. Now suddenly she wanted it — chains and ropes and bangles — a jewelry box that chimed when you opened the lid —

blouses with open necks instead of T-shirts and crew sweaters.

Anya tied a long, dark cranberry red belt around her waist and adjusted the tulip flare of her long skirt. She looked like a magazine ad. She was every adjective: romantic, tailored, seductive, and scholarly all at one time.

They went to breakfast, remembering to walk down the stairs. No guests appeared, although it was just after Labor Day weekend, and Christina thought if there were any hope of winter guests, there would surely be early September guests.

Christina was used to a huge breakfast. Her mother generally rose at four A.M. to serve the fishermen going out for the day. Today a single piece of dry whole wheat toast, a small bowl of cold cereal onto which half a banana had been sliced, and a tiny glass of orange juice were laid in front of her.

Christina got up and poked around in the refrigerator for jam to spread on her toast. She was leaning way down inside to inspect the back of the bottom shelf when something hard and cold jabbed her in the middle of her back. It felt like the tip of a gun, or a knitting needle. It dug between two of her vertebrae. Christina straightened up slowly.

Mrs. Shevvington removed her long, thick fingernail from Christina's spine. "Too much sugar is bad for you, Christina. Learn to eat your toast dry."

Mrs. Shevvington was wearing a royal blue suit with a lacy blouse. It covered her thick body as if she had zipped it off a store mannequin and zipped herself back in. She hardly seemed to be wearing the suit; it was just hanging there: It could as easily have been hanging on a closet door. Mrs. Shevvington's hand was still in midair, like a sea gull drifting on wind currents. The fingernail that had left a dent in her flesh was thick and hooked, like a hawk's toe.

Fingers, thought Christina.

She tried to remember last night, and Anya, and the voices Anya had heard. But the memories were slippery, like seaweed.

She had had no supper. Now she was supposed to have dry toast. Christina had a large appetite. "We have lots of time," she said, glancing at the clock. "I could make waffles. Who wants waffles?"

Mrs. Shevvington moved closer to the girl. Under the protection of her shirt and sweater, Christina shivered. If that fingernail had touched her bare skin, it would have slit her spinal cord.

Yarning, she thought, why am I yarning every minute now? I have to get a grip on myself! It's only a fingernail, she's only a seventh-grade teacher.

How could Christina have English with this woman? What could she ever write — what paragraph, what essay — that this woman would understand? What book would Mrs. Shevvington ever assign that Christina would want to read?

"Christina, I don't hear the others complaining about a perfectly nutritious breakfast."

Michael was crunching away at his cereal. He had dressed as carefully as the girls. He obviously wanted to look like Blake. He had untied the laces in his dock shoes, wound them in upright spirals, and gone sockless — this year's way to establish style.

Anya, who never ate anyway, was sipping from a thimble of orange juice. This was her kind of meal.

Benj was eating Anya's dry toast for her, having already wolfed down her cereal and banana.

"I'll cook the waffles myself," Christina said. "It wouldn't be a bother to anybody. I'll clean up, too. And I'm a very good cook. My mother taught me everything."

"She did not teach you manners," Mrs. Shevvington said. "It would be most unfortunate if, because of a bad attitude, you were not able to board here after all, and had to be moved *alone* to some other location." She smiled at Christina. None of the others could have seen that smile. Christina wished she had never seen the smile, either. It was the war smile. Just try to oppose me, Christina, it said.

Board alone. What did that mean? Without Anya and Michael and Benj? Then she really would have no friends!

Christina tried to eat the toast dry. It crumbled in her throat. She tried to enjoy the banana. It was too ripe and slimy.

Michael said to her, "Now don't let them get you crying. Those town kids like to pick on island kids."

"I never cry," said Christina, who was very close to it.

Anya gave her a queer, tight smile. "You might today," she said.

"They can be mean," Michael told her. "Everybody needs somebody to pick on."

"Nobody picks on me," Christina said.

"You mean nobody ever *has* picked on you, Chrissie," Benj told her. "You haven't experienced it yet. You're going to experience it today. All week. All September."

"Some of us," said Anya, "experience it all year, year after year."

People picked on Anya? How could anybody look at Anya and not feel a rush of pleasure in her beauty and her presence?

But there was one silver lining in this. Michael cared. For all his summer speeches about how if Christina tried to hold his hand he would flatten her, here he was, trying to give her courage.

"Now, you will need house keys," said Mrs. Shevvington. She handed each of them a shiny new duplicate. "The front door is to be kept locked at all times."

Christina held her key, feeling its unfiled edges, staring at the jagged profile. I'll get home first, she thought, and open that huge green door myself. I'll be the grown-up.

Mrs. Shevvington gave them instructions for cleaning up the kitchen. Then she made it clear that although Mr. Shevvington had a car (and had left much earlier) and although she too had a car (and was leaving now) the children were not going to be offered rides with either Shevvington. "You children have two choices. You may walk. It is only a quarter mile." She filled her lungs with air, making an exercise out of it, as if she were doing push-ups. "Good for you. Brisk. Or you may go down Breakneck Hill and catch the school bus at its last stop by the Mobil gas station." She waved good-bye as if she were a half mile from the children. "Have a satisfactory first day." She walked out of the house.

"Satisfactory?" exclaimed Christina. "That's the best wish she can give us? What happened to *wonderful*, *terrific*, *friend-filled*, or *rewarding*?"

The others did not pick up her lines. They neither joked nor contradicted. Was school so awful that Anya, Benj, and Michael already knew the best it could be was satisfactory?

Or were they on Mrs. Shevvington's side? Did they, too, think Christina had a bad attitude?

The girls got light canvas jackets because it did not look as if the day would warm up; the boys scorned protection from the elements and sauntered outdoors in shirtsleeves. Anya had a lovely briefcase with her initials on it, and pockets for pens, pencils, and a calculator. Her purse was a tiny dark red leather bag on a long thin spaghetti strap, which exactly matched her belt. Christina had only a five-subject spiral notebook with a yellow cover, and two pencils crammed into the spiral. The boys carried nothing. "Wait for me," Christina said. "I have to get my purse."

She raced upstairs, taking the steep steps two at a time. *This* was how stairs should be climbed! Her purse, so carefully bought with summer earnings, was not something she could leave behind. She had waited all these years to be old enough to have a purse at all.

But back downstairs, her precious purse felt clunky and dumb next to Anya's tiny bag. She was not used to holding it and it banged against her and took up space.

Outside Benj checked to be sure the door had locked behind him. He attached his house key to his Swiss army knife and jammed that into his pocket. Michael fastened his to his belt. Anya had a tiny zip pocket on her tiny purse into which she slipped her key. Christina's mother had made her a key ring, her name embroidered onto canvas in a leather oblong like a luggage tag. Christina and her mother had been so proud of the key ring. Now Christina thought, It's too big. And dumb. Nobody else bothers with anything like that.

She was suddenly horribly afraid.

Afraid of all those other children, all those rooms and corridors, all those times when she would have to walk alone, sit alone, eat alone. And be different, with her dumb fat key tag, and her dumb fat purse, and her strange tri-colored hair the other kids would say she dyed.

Wind lifted out of Candle Cove, billowing Anya's skirt and making a black storm cloud of her hair. Christina and the boys in their jeans and sweaters were as untouched by the wind as if it had steered around them. The first day comes only once, she told herself. No other day can be as bad as the first one.

So tomorrow will be fine. Stop being jittery. Don't yarn. Don't make it worse by exaggerating. Mrs. Shevvington is right; aim for a satisfactory day.

Christina bumped her fingertips along the wire fence that kept people from falling into Candle Cove.

Down in the mud flats, in almost exactly the same place as the day before, stood somebody in a brown wet suit. There was no water there to swim in. There was no boat to get into or out of. There was no bucket for clams. It was just a wet suit, gleaming.

It walked in the children's direction fluidly, as if being poured. Mud sucked on its feet. Christina could hear the sucking. She could see the mud, reaching up above the toes, grabbing the ankles. The wet suit came to a stop. It lifted its right hand, very slowly, very high, and beckoned.

"Listen to his fingers," whispered Anya. "It's not a wave. Not a hello. *Come here*, say the fingers. *Come down here and drown with me.*"

Out in the Atlantic, the waiting ocean chuckled and hissed.

The wet suit raised the other arm, as if to embrace them.

Christina was already suffocating in the embrace of her own fear and loneliness. She wanted to be hugged. The wet suit would hug her. She listened to the fingers, like Anya.

Come here, said the fingers. *Come here and drown with me.*

But her sneaker tip hit the fence and a button on her jacket caught on the wires.

I almost walked over the edge, thought Christina Romney, disengaging her button. Some guy down there waves, and I start believing Anya's yarns. She said the sea knew we were here. She said the sea kept count. She said the sea wants one of us.

Down in the mud the arms leaned toward them, longingly.

Christina wrenched her eyes off the wet suit.

Very slowly a car drove up Breakneck Hill. It was tiny and bright red, gleaming new, as if the driver were on a test drive from the showroom. It was shaped like a long, thin triangle, with the pointed end ready for take-off. The headlights were hidden under slanting hoods. Inside, the upholstery was even redder.

The driver stuck a casual sleeve out the window, followed by a casual turn of the head.

It was Blake.

How handsome he was! A catalog Maine model featured among the hunting equipment and camping accessories.

"Hi, Anya," said Blake. He did not smile. His heavy eyebrows lay neatly on his tanned face, and his deep set eyes matched them perfectly, as if they too had been ordered from the catalog. "Would you like to ride to school with me, Anya?" he said. He was nervous, as if she might say no.

He planned this, Christina thought, filled with romantic appreciation. He timed it. He probably test-drove the route so he'd arrive at just the right moment. Or maybe he's been sitting at the bottom of the hill, waiting to see the front door open, and Anya, whom he loves, emerge!

Anya smiled at Blake. Her whole face smiled — even her body seemed to smile. Shyly she touched her stormy hair, and the wind responded by covering her fingers as well as her face. From beneath the black mist of her own hair, Anya whispered, "I'd love to, Blake."

Blake's smile broke through his face like the sun through the fog, dazzling them. He bit his lip, a childlike expression that Anya returned with a wild, loving laugh. In this world of smart cars and fine clothes, only Anya could make Blake happy. Christina could tell by their lips, which were desperate with the need to laugh, kiss, and beg at the same time. Anya danced around the car to slip in beside Blake. He leaned toward her, as if to kiss her, and she held her face up, but in the end he did not, and Christina was disappointed. Instead Blake pushed the pedal to the floor and took off in a squeal of tires. From the back the car had no shape at all; its triangle was pointed away from them and it was nothing but a red cube.

Michael and Benj walked on. Michael's posture said, This is where I stop knowing you, Christina. Remember not to bother me.

They've abandoned me, she thought. I'll have to walk into the school alone. When I go up those steps, I won't have a single friend on the American continent.

Alone.

It was a word so horrible she seemed to hear it in the waves, repeating over and over, saying, *You're alone, Christina, alone, alone, alone.*

The school itself was plain; brick rooms squatting around a courtyard. But the front steps were pink granite from Burning Fog Isle — fifty feet wide, impressive as a state capitol. In fair weather, half the school sat on the steps to eat lunch. What if hundreds of teenagers, all with their best friends, leaned against each other, talked to each other, shared with each other — but left Christina alone? What if she, and only she, had to stand in the sun, shunned and unwanted?

Clutching her notebook and purse like a sword and lance, Christina looked back at the Cove.

It was empty. There was nobody in a wet suit.

There was nobody there at all but a little cormorant, drying its wings.

Chapter 5

Christina had math first. The teacher, Miss Schuyler, was a plain young woman with odd, old-fashioned braids. I like her, Christina thought. Oh, please, let her like me!

Miss Schuyler said how lovely it was to have new faces this year. "Let's welcome Brandi, who's moved here from Boston," Miss Schuyler said, pointing to a little dark girl cringing in the back. The class smiled. Everybody said, "Hi, Brandi. Glad to have you, Brandi." The little girl stopped cringing.

"And Kevin, who was here up through third grade, moved away, and is now back," Miss Schuyler went on, pointing to a tall, very thin boy in a sweatshirt so large it nearly touched his knees. The class welcomed Kevin.

Christina braced herself. Her purse, sitting on the desk, looked fat and stupid. Nobody else had spiral notebooks. Their paper was in three ring binders with impressive fold-out pockets and zips.

Nobody else wore brand new jeans. All their jeans were old.

"And our third new face is Christina, who lives on Burning Fog Isle, and is boarding on the mainland for the school year!"

There was no teasing.

Everybody looked as if this were the most interesting, romantic thing they had ever heard.

Miss Schuyler said it had always been her personal fantasy to live on an island, but she was not brave enough: It took courage to live on an island, she said, and she knew through the year they would find Christina a person of courage.

Nobody laughed at this. They looked awed.

Two girls asked Christina to be sure and sit with them at lunch.

Next Christina had science. Both the girls who had asked her for lunch — Vicki and Gretchen — were in science with her, and she sat between them. The science teacher said how well prepared island children always were; it put the rest of the class to shame.

Nobody teased Christina about that either; they looked respectful of Christina's superior knowledge.

Gym was what Christina feared most. Her knowledge of team games was almost zero. She discovered that nobody else knew how to hold a hockey stick, either.

She was as athletic as any of them.

It's going to be all right, Christina thought. I'm going to make it.

Changing classes was not as scary as she expected. Most seventh-graders stayed together, and the classrooms weren't spread very far apart. Choosing a desk wasn't awful; nobody saved seats for best friends; they just walked in and slid down. All desks were modern and slick, seats attached like one-room schoolhouse desks. Christina found it difficult to get in and out of them. Everybody else was graceful. Except the boys, who kicked things, stuck their feet out, wrapped their ankles around themselves, and honked like geese.

Christina was fascinated by the boys.

So many of them!

They were all like Michael, with immense feet and hands and noses. They were noisier than Michael, though, and had specialties Michael did not. The boys showed off their skills at hiccuping, burping, and jumping on each other's feet. This was what you were supposed to fall in love with? Where were the boys like Blake? She examined her classmates for potential Blakes and decided there were none. Seventh grade had a full complement of creeps, weirdos, future criminals, and nerds.

At lunch it turned out that Vicki and Gretch were fashionable. They were "in" — a phenomenon Christina had read about but never experienced, as the island had so few children. Other giggling seventh-graders angled for the chance to sit at the same table. Vicki and Gretch were given extra desserts. Vicki and Gretch's opinions were sought and their jokes laughed at.

The girls were much more attractive than the boys. They were neater, cleaner, and prettier.

Christina nevertheless could not take her eyes off the boys. How annoying that the boys sat at their own tables and the girls sat at others. Christina wanted to be next to the boys.

She was full of second-day-of-school resolutions. No purse, better notebook, memorize everybody's names, scruffy jeans.

"If you're not going to eat your Jell-O, can I have it?" Gretch asked. "I love it with whipped cream."

Christina handed Gretch her Jell-O. She wouldn't have eaten it anyway because she liked only dark-colored Jell-O (raspberry, strawberry) and never touched light-colored Jell-O (lime, lemon). It was a small price to pay for Gretch smiling at her, for being "in" like Vicki and Gretch, for sitting at what was obviously the best table.

The only thing wrong with lunch was that she did not pay for it.

Mrs. Shevvington had handed her a blue ticket to exchange for a hot lunch. Christina noticed that about a quarter of the students had these; the rest brought bag lunches, or paid money to buy a hot lunch.

"How come I have this blue ticket?" Christina asked Gretch.

"Because you're poor," Gretch said. "Island kids are always poor. The state is paying for your lunch."

For the first time Christina saw that Gretch, too, was dressed in catalog Maine. That while Christina's jeans were from a sale rack in a discount store, bought on a mainland shopping trip in July, Gretch's jeans had a brand name Christina recognized from full-page ads in *Seventeen* magazine. I might be able to afford the three-ring binder, thought Christina, but not the jeans.

She wanted jeans like Gretch's.

It was the first time in Christina's life that she had lusted after a brand name. She hated her own boring, unstylish jeans. They embarrassed her, they hung wrong, and they were too blue. She resented her parents for being poor and living where they didn't know anything about seventh-grade fashion.

Anya walked over to Christina's table.

An honor roll, drama club, soprano solo, tennis team, senior girl — pausing at lunch to chat with a seventh-grader? Even Christina, who knew nothing of the social life of schools, knew this was remarkable. Senior high kids ate on one side of the cafeteria and lowly junior high kids on the other. Nobody crossed the invisible lines, not with their feet, their speech, or their eyes.

Gretch and Vicki were awestruck. Their giggles were silenced. Their Jell-O spoons hung motionless. Anya had never looked so beautiful. The eyes of all the seniors and juniors followed her, and so, in person, did Blake. Now the younger girls almost swooned. Blake was perfect. Anya was perfect. Anya and Blake together were twice as perfect.

At first Christina thought Anya had come over to make Christina look good and stop any teasing that might have begun. But Anya's eyes caught Christina's with a strange, dark desperation. Anya was not crossing the cafeteria lines to be sure Christina was surviving her first day, nor to borrow a dime for a phone call, nor to give her a message — but because Anya was not okay.

Christina did not know what to offer. She could not imagine what had gone wrong for Anya.

Anya held her arms out for comfort.

Blake caught up to Anya. Certainly Blake wasn't upset. Laughing, he took both of Anya's outstretched hands and twirled her away, like a dance partner. The seventh-grade girls sighed in delicious envy. "Do you see a lot of Blake?" breathed Gretch. "He's so wonderful! He's so handsome!"

"What's it like on that island of yours?" Vicki asked. Vicki was very tan, and wore a white cotton knit sweater, which made her look even tanner. Her light brown hair was absolutely straight, and it swung when she moved. She had a tourist look to her; she was the day tripper they scorned on the island.

"Oh, you know," Christine said, "just a rock and some sea gulls."

She flushed with shame. She loved Burning Fog. Why had she made it sound like a garbage dump?

"I *adore* sea gulls," said Gretch. "They're so *beautiful* and *pure*. I love how they tilt in the wind." Gretch had blonde hair, cut exactly like Vicki's, and they had a habit of tilting themselves toward each other, so their brown and yellow hair swung together and then swung apart.

"I don't think pure is the word," said Christina. "You should see them with baby ducks and baby terns. Why, one sea gull could goffle up a whole brood."

Gretch's blonde eyebrows lifted like punctuation marks. *"Goffle?"* she said, starting to laugh. She turned to Vicki, who giggled with her. They tilted hair. "Goffle. That's so cute. What other cute little words do you know, Christina?"

Christina said lamely, "I mean eat. Sea gulls eat anything." She would not tell them how her mother took the kitchen garbage, eggshells, crusts, and scrapings off plates to the top of the cliff, where sea gulls would swoop down like Roman gladiators.

Once they stood up from the table, junior high etiquette allowed the boys to join them. This turned the girls arch and silly. Christina did not know how to be arch and silly. One boy claimed to be able to spit tobacco farther than anybody, but as the cafeteria proctor was approaching, he could not substantiate this claim. One girl said out on Burning Fog Isle even the girls chewed tobacco. "I bet Christina can spit as far as you can," she said. "That's probably what she does when she's not canning fish."

Everybody laughed.

Another boy said he had been to Burning Fog Isle himself several times. Each summer his parents liked a day trip and a picnic on Burning Fog. Christina did not tell him what she thought of day trippers, but he was not so polite to her. He said he did not think much of islanders. He said they charged too much for soft drinks and yelled when you touched their silly dock.

It was probably Christina's mother who had sold him the soft drink. It was probably Frankie's dock.

Michael had told her to laugh it off. Christina could not find any laughs. But it was the other seventh-graders who laughed, closing in on Christina, talking louder and louder.

She had been afraid of being alone. Now she was afraid of being in the center.

"What's your house like?" said the boy. He had a funny, knowing smile. She felt wary, the way she would around lobster claws. "Is it one of those little shacks that always needs a coat of paint?" he said.

Vicki and Gretch giggled. "Jonah," they said, warningly — but coaxingly, so they could get credit for telling him to stop, but yet not stop him.

"It's a cottage," Christina said.

Jonah smiled triumphantly. "I know which cottage, too," he said to the rest of the seventh grade. "Christina's cottage has thirty-two rooms."

Gretch and Vicki looked impressed. They blended their hair together like a fence against strangers.

Jonah said, "And notice that, nevertheless, Christina is getting free lunch. Another welfare cheat. Welcome to our midst."

In English, Christina did indeed have Mrs. Shevvington.

The manners in her room were markedly different. There was no jostling or kidding. Even the boys behaved like human beings, without spitting, tripping their friends, or imitating tomcats in heat.

Mrs. Shevvington stood in front of the class, and the class sat in front of Mrs. Shevvington, and nothing else happened. Mrs. Shevvington gave a lecture while twenty-four children took notes.

When Christina picked up her pencil to take notes, her fingers smudged the page, and she left a sweaty palm print where the pencil couldn't write. Class seemed to last forever, and yet when the bell rang nobody jumped up. They waited until Mrs. Shevvington excused them. Then they walked quietly out of the classroom, just as Christina had to walk quietly down the stairs at the Schooner Inne.

In the hall Vicki and Gretch walked on either side of Christina as if the cafeteria scenes had never happened and they were a trio of best girlfriends.

"What's it like living with the Shevvingtons?" said Vicki. "Mr. Shevvington is so handsome, don't you adore him? If he weren't a hundred years old, I would have a crush on him. But Mrs. Shevvington is so dull, isn't she? It's like being in first grade every year, absolutely nothing happens. Oh, well, at least she's sweet. Her first name is Candy. I think it fits perfectly, don't you?"

If they thought I was yarning about sea gulls, she thought, they'd never believe me about the Shevvingtons.

She walked down the hall, smelling school: a chalk-sweat-paper-floorwax-mimeograph smell she had never smelled before. As distinctive as low tide; the kind of smell you would never get wrong, you would remember all your life.

"Listen," said Gretch, smiling. "Don't be upset

about Jonah finding out you're a welfare cheat, Christina. He's really into honesty, that's all." Vicki and Gretch escorted Christina on down the long hall, telling her that the next class was art. "You'll hate art," Vicki said. "Everybody hates art. The art teacher stinks."

"I am not a welfare cheat," Christina said. "I'm into honesty, too. We don't own the cottage, we just — "

"And don't call it a cottage, either," said Jonah, coming up behind them. "Anybody who lives in a thirty-two room house lives in a palace. And then you're rude to the mainland tourists who end up paying for your free school lunch as well as buying your overpriced soda. It's disgusting."

Christina belted him in the mouth. When he staggered back, unprepared, she belted him a second time. This was so satisfying she was ready to do it a third time, when Miss Schuyler responded to the screams of Vicki and Gretch.

"That island girl hit him first!" yelled all the witnesses.

Miss Schuyler grabbed Christina by her sweater sleeve and Jonah by his pink oxford collar. "I cannot believe this," hissed the math teacher. "The very first day of school, and you are starting fist fights. We do not do this kind of thing here, Christina. Nor, Jonah Bergeron, do we fight little girls who are here for the very first day of their lives."

Jonah snorted. "Some little girl," he said.

Miss Schuyler hauled them down to the principal's office. They went through an outer office full of high counters and secretaries. Miss Schuyler knocked hard on a yellow door blackened around the handle with fingerprints, and pushed into Mr. Shevvington's office.

When Jonah finished his explanation there was silence in the room. Christina was aware of tall filing cabinets, piles of papers, books tumbling sideways, and an open window through which came the smell of the fish cannery. Mr. Shevvington seemed not to be a part of his office, any more than his wife had been a part of her clothing. He was simply handsome and silvery and sad. He fixed his eyes on Christina, and the eyes never blinked.

He'll call my parents, she thought. I've been away from home a day and a half, and look at me. In trouble with everybody.

Mr. Shevvington's voice was gentle, and yet rough, like a luxury car driving slowly over pebbles. "Christina," he said sadly, "I am so disappointed in you."

Christina's heart began to pound hideously, as if at thirteen she were going to have a heart attack. "I got mad at Jonah," she whispered. "I'm sorry." She felt as worthless as an empty soda can by the side of the road.

Mr. Shevvington sighed. Then he turned to Jonah. "Christina's father is caretaker of a millionaire's mansion. They don't have access to the house, but live in the servants' quarters because that's what they are, Jonah. Servants. Christina needs free lunch more than anybody else. I don't want you to gossip about her situation, but you might let people know that Christina is the kind of Maine native who knows poverty firsthand. So although yes, she's on welfare, no, she is not a welfare cheat."

Christina felt punched. "We have never been on welfare! My mother runs a restaurant."

"Her mother serves toast and coffee to lobstermen from a little shack near the harbor," said Mr. Shevvington to Jonah. "Now I want you two to be friends. That is your assignment for the fall, Jonah. You take Christina on as a friend and help her steer a safe passage among the rocks of junior high."

"Yes, sir," said Jonah. He was staring down at his shoes. Christina stared there, too. Yet another example of catalog Maine, only this time it was hunting boots, which most certainly had never been taken hunting.

I hate them! thought Christina. I hate them all. "I am not on welfare," she said.

"What do you think a free lunch is?" said Jonah.

Christina flung back her head to shout, *Then I'll never take free lunch again!* when she realized that her parents did not, in fact, have money to send for buying hot lunches, that Mrs. Shevvington was unlikely to buy her boxes of apple juice and Twinkies when the state would supply it free, and that she did not, at thirteen, earn any money herself.

Mr. Shevvington ordered her to apologize to Jonah.

"I'm sorry," muttered Christina without looking at him.

Jonah was excused to return to class, with a little

note from Mr. Shevvington to carry to his teacher. Mr. Shevvington's handwriting was delicate enough for wedding invitations. His muscular fingers did not look right making such thin, graceful shapes.

The principal dropped back down into his chair and smiled at Christina.

Christina had thought she would never smile again, but Mr. Shevvington's smile was so kind. Little by little Christina's face and mouth relaxed, and slowly she managed a smile of her own. The worst was over. Mr. Shevvington said that junior high could be something of a shock. Children age thirteen, he explained, were barbarians. He knew Christina was not, of course, but she was not used to the pressure of a whole grade around her. She would have to be calm, and pliant, and let them all have their way.

Christina did not see why they should always have their way. She didn't feel like being calm and pliant. She felt like belting Jonah again. But she did not say so. This is good practice, she told herself, and she made herself look pliant, like a flower stem in the wind.

"While you're here, Christina, why don't you fill out this form we will need to guide you through your school career."

Forms! she thought eagerly.

Christina loved to fill in blanks. Mostly she sent away for folders and leaflets about anything at all, just to get mail. This would be a *real* form.

Christina accepted the clipboard Mr. Shevvington gave her to write on and the pen he passed her to write with. With each item, she felt more like somebody too poor or too stupid to have brought her own. "My things are still on the floor in the hall where Miss Schuyler grabbed me," she said.

Mr. Shevvington nodded as if he did not believe her, but was willing to accept Christina's fibs to save her pride.

I won't cry, she told herself. I never cry. I won't now.

She took the pen purposefully. She could make her script just as beautiful as his. She'd show him.

The form was entitled *Getting to Know You*. Computer generated sixteenth notes floated in the margins, like a happy song. Christina filled in name, address, parents' occupations. Then she looked at the questions. Her brow wrinkled. They were very odd questions.

"How come I didn't get this in homeroom along with the medical forms?" she asked Mr. Shevvington.

"It's only for new students."

"But all the students in my grade are new," she protested, "starting junior high for the first time."

Mr. Shevvington wound a pencil around in his fingers like a baton twirler. "Christina, I hope this is not a harbinger of things to come. Do you have difficulty with authority? Are you going to be continually presenting problems and arguing? Mrs. Shevvington and I decided to overlook both last night and this morning, because we know how nervous you must be, an island child away from home for the first time — but I am beginning to have doubts about your ability to handle yourself."

Her hand grew sweaty around the pen. The metal chair poked her back like Mrs. Shevvington's fingernail. It's true, she thought. Nobody else argued. Nobody else got in a fistfight. Michael told me to laugh when they teased. I never even tried to laugh. I just socked Jonah.

Mr. Shevvington said gently, "Christina, I want you to think about counseling. We have a wonderful guidance department here. We have a social worker who understands troubled adolescents very well. I want you to consider working with her to sort out your emotional problems. Of course it will be your decision. We won't force you into anything."

Emotional problems? Christina thought. Me?

She had always been the granite of her family, the old strong stock of the island. It was Anya who was the endangered species, the fragile one.

Or was it?

"Now fill out the form," said Mr. Shevvington gently. His eyes were warm, soft: eyes to wrap a child in comfort.

"But these questions — " began Christina. She wet her lips.

"Will help us understand you," the principal said.

Christina lowered her eyes to the page. The letters were soothing; the alphabet never changed; the white rectangle of the pages never changed.

She tried to breathe evenly.

What are you afraid of? asked the first question. *Circle all that apply.*

Rats?
Darkness?
Being laughed at?
Pain?
Acid?
Failure?
Being alone?

Most of the time, Christina Romney thought, I am afraid of nothing.

Some of the time, I am afraid of everything.

But I am not telling anybody which I'm afraid of, or when.

"I won't fill this out, Mr. Shevvington."

"You must, Christina, dear."

"No."

The word sat alone, like an island in the sea.

There was a long silence. Christina did not look at his eyes. The eyes, like the beckoning hand of the wet suit, might force her into something.

The silence lasted and lasted. What would happen in art without her? Would Jonah be there even now, telling them all how poverty-stricken she was? How her parents were nothing but servants? It wasn't true. Her father was an excellent tennis player. Her mother was an excellent cook.

"Then you may go," Mr. Shevvington said. "But I want you to know that I am your friend. All I want is to help you. And Christina — "

She set the clipboard and pen on his desk and backed out of the office.

" — you desperately need help."

Chapter 6

After school Christina went to look for Anya, Michael, and Benj, but it was Jonah she found. Or actually, Jonah who found Christina.

"Get lost," said Christina. "I don't want any friends by marching orders from the principal."

Jonah said nervously. "I have to do what he says."

"Why? I won't rat on you. If he ever asks, I'll say you're very attentive, and helpful in every way. Now get lost."

Jonah stuck with her. "He's watching," whispered Jonah. "Let me walk with you as far as Breakneck Hill." The heavy hunting boots clumped along with her. Twice Jonah looked over his shoulder.

Twice Christina forced herself to look straight ahead.

Jonah was slightly shorter than Christina, but boys usually were at that age. All of him was thin: even his lips and his eyelids were thin. But it was not as thin as girls can be — anorexic. It was thin for the moment: Tomorrow, or next week, Jonah would grow six inches and gain seventy-five pounds. His hands were much too large for his seventh-grade body; his feet big as a clown's; his teeth too square. "You have funny hair," Jonah said. "Is it dyed?"

"No, it isn't dyed. And what kind of name is Jonah, anyway?" added Christina, getting in a dig of her own. "It sounds like a graveyard name to me."

Jonah stared at her.

Too late she remembered this was yet another island saying Anya had forbidden her to use.

Names fascinated Christina. So far in seventh grade she had met Kimberly, Jennie, Krystyn, Sable, Brandi, Vicki, and Gretch. But generations back, Christina's ancestors had names like Florence, Nellie, Phoebe, and HepsiBeth. They were in the graveyard on Burning Fog Isle, where their stones were routinely checked by graveyard buffs who wanted a rubbing of the angel on HepsiBeth's stone. Christina had always thought HepsiBeth sounded like a soft drink — Pepsi Cola, Coca Cola, HepsiBeth.

"We always give our cats graveyard names," said Christina to Jonah. "Off the old gravestones. One year the litter was Emmaline, Tristram, Jethro, Jemima, Dorcas, and Abiah. Jonah sounds like a good cat's name."

Jonah said, "You're weird, Christina."

"Good. Then you don't have to be friends with me. Forget your marching orders." Christina walked away from Jonah. Then she remembered something and turned around again. "There is one way you can help me. But you can't tell Mr. Shevvington about it."

Jonah did not look thrilled about something for which he got no credit.

"I want to see the house where Anya lived last year. It's in this neighborhood somewhere." If I get in even more trouble, she thought, the Shevvingtons will send me away. Probably there.

Her head ached with the day's events. She felt as if it would take all autumn to think through what had happened. And in only a little while she had to face the Shevvingtons again, and Anya and Michael and Benj. They would all know about the fistfight with Jonah.

Jonah took her down a narrow street, away from the cute little tourist-trade, sailor-trade shops. Past car repair places stinking of oil, and old sagging warehouses with weeds growing in the cracks of the buildings.

He pointed to a thick, squat house with seaweed-green asphalt siding. It was a house where poor people lived; where the smell of cabbage clung to the torn wallpaper and the ugly carpet curled up and collected spiders. Where there would be only one bathroom, and its tub would be pockmarked and its shower curtain moldy. There was no yard, no view of the sea, no color, and no wind.

Christina shuddered.

I, from my island of wild grass and roses, of leaping salt spray and seabirds floating in air currents — living *there*?

"Creepy, huh?" Jonah said. "Aren't you glad you live in Schooner Inne this year?"

Christina thought, Why did the Shevvingtons decide to take us? They don't have any other guests. I don't think they're going to have other guests. I think we'll live in the attic and they'll live on the second floor and nobody else will come. Ever. Anya says we're living with the Shevvingtons because they're so kind. Vicki and Gretch adore Mr. Shevvington. I don't think they're kind.

She remembered what the tourist on Frankie's boat had said. *Don't they look like ancient island princesses, marked out for sacrifice? Sent away for the sake of the islanders, to be given to the sea?*

"What's it like in the cupola?" Jonah said.

"I haven't been up there yet."

He was amazed. "A girl that slugs boys the first day of school hasn't explored the best part of the sea captain's house yet?" he said. "That's where the sea captain's wife stood when she dove to her death."

"Couldn't have," said Christina, who wanted never to agree with Jonah about anything. "It's all glassed in."

Jonah shrugged. "She didn't care if she got cut by a little glass, did she? She just jumped through it."

Christina was horrified. She had never thought of that.

Why had Mr. Shevvington smiled, saying, "I know," when Anya promised to do anything he asked?

Why had Anya said "The sea keeps count. The sea is a mathematician. The sea wants one of us"?

Jonah and Christina waited for the light to change at the bottom of Breakneck Hill. The waves crashed in Candle Cove. Six cars crossed the Singing Bridge, and the open metal floor of the bridge hummed loudly as the rubber tires spun over it. Christina had always loved the Singing Bridge.

"It sings when somebody drowns, you know," said Jonah.

"I've lived here all my life and I've never heard that," Christina said.

"Huh. You've lived on Burning Fog Isle all your life, not this town. I suppose town is pretty exciting for you, huh? Must be real quiet on that island once the tourists are gone."

"It's never quiet. The sea crashes, the gulls scream, the motors of the boats roar, chain saws cut wood, anchor chains rattle, shutters bang, the wind whistles — "

"Okay, okay, it's noisy on the island. I meant people."

"I do not," said Christina sharply, "consider tourists such as yourself to be *people*, Jonah."

She stalked up Breakneck Hill, not an easy thing to do. It was too steep for stalking. The glass of the cupola caught the sun and blinded her.

Neither of the Shevvingtons could be home from school yet. Christina would climb the cupola.

This had been the worst day of her entire life.

And she had no mother to greet her with something yummy, hot from the oven; no Dolly to share it with; no VCR to put her favorite movie in; no litter of kittens to play with on the kitchen floor.

Christina had never expected to be homesick, and certainly not the first day. Her sides hurt, as if she had cramps from running.

She unlocked the huge green door, shut it quietly behind her, and went inside.

No guests sat in the formal living room; no guests snacked in the formal dining room. The kitchen was dark and silent. The dingy den was empty.

Christina carried her books up to her room.

She got to the top of the stairs and the bedroom door was closed.

She distinctly remembered leaving it open that morning.

Mrs. Shevvington certainly hadn't gone in; she had left for school before they had.

Inside the room Christina could hear breathing.

She set down her book bag. Then she picked it up again to use its weight as a weapon.

The breath came in little huffs like a panting animal.

She swallowed. She cracked the door. No black wet nose of a dog or cat came through the crack. The breathing continued. Like somebody blowing out candles on a birthday cake. Like —

Oh, it's just the tide! thought Christina, utterly disgusted with herself.

She flung open the door, and the bedroom, of course, was completely empty. The huffing continued. Christina crossed the room to close the window, from which a sea wind must have blown the door shut.

"You be quiet, you cove, you," she muttered out the window.

She considered having a cry. Girls in books often curled up alone in the corners of their rooms and wept till they felt better. Christina had never felt bad enough about anything that she wanted to cry at all, let alone curl up for a weep. This was the kind of day that did it, then. If I'm going to do that, she thought, I'll need supplies. Kleenex. And a book in case I get bored.

"Christina, Christina!"

She jerked away from the window and ran to the stairs. Anya — Anya must be hurt — the wet suit — the tide —

"I'm so glad you're home," said Anya, running up the stairs. "Chrissie, I've had the worst day of my life. I have to tell you about it."

She hauled Christina back into the bedroom before Christina could tell her about the huffing, and flung them both on their beds. "Nobody has ever had a worse day," said Anya dramatically. She ran all ten fingers up into her hair and pretended to scalp herself.

The huffing stopped.

It's listening instead, thought Christina. Like me.

"First of all, Blake's parents say I'm nothing but a wharf rat and they want better for Blake."

A wharf rat. Girls who worked on the docks, knee

deep in fish heads and motor oil, and lost all their teeth before they were twenty-five. Girls who worked in the factories and had babies before they were sixteen and ate ten jelly doughnuts at a time because nobody cared whether they got fat and ugly.

"Anya, you could never be a wharf rat."

"That's what Blake says. But if we see each other, we have to sneak. Christina, I've never sneaked in my life. Blake's parents even told the Shevvingtons they don't want him to date me. They didn't actually order him not to, but they made it clear that he will upset them if he does."

Christina knew how it felt to be shunned. "Wait till you hear about *my* day," she said, settling in cross-legged on top of her mother's quilt.

"No. I'm not finished yet. Then I found out that the guidance department re-did my academic schedule. They put me in Public Speaking, Chrissie! Five days a week. Public Speaking. Do you know what that is? Each kid has to get up once a week and give an assigned talk. Out loud." Anya flung herself backward on the mattress and bounced. "When I filled out my form for Mr. Shevvington," she said, "I marked speaking in front of an audience as the thing I feared most. And here I am, in it. Mr. Shevvington says it's good for me. He says I have to learn to face my fears."

The huffing moved inside Christina's head like a warning signal. Christina said slowly, "What form?"

"The one we all had to fill out. The personality

one for guidance. Those questions were so awful. What did you put for that one?"

Christina's hands were cold. "I didn't fill that one out. I'm not afraid of anything." *Liar, liar, house on fire*, ran the nursery song in her head.

Anya popped up off the mattress. "You lucky thing. I might have known. Benj and Michael aren't afraid of anything either. They just laughed when Mr. Shevvington gave them the form."

"I thought the form was for new students."

"No, no, the *form* is new."

Christina was gasping again. I must have asthma, she thought. Great. One day away from the island and I need glasses and medication.

"Guess what my first speech has to be."

"What?"

" 'Describe your house.' "

"Oh, but Anya, that's an easy topic! You can tell all about the sea captain, and his bride, and the stairs, and the dark, dank, dingy den where we are forced to watch television."

Anya unexpectedly flung herself over the gap between the two beds and hugged Christina. "Oh, Chrissie, you lifesaver! I was thinking of my real house! My shack with the broken window panes and the chickens that live in the rusted-out station wagon and the privy for when the plumbing fails. I could never tell all these mainland kids about how I really live! Not when Blake's parents already think I'm a wharf rat!" She huffed a breath of relief. In Christina's ears the huff echoed and re-echoed,

Candle Cove in their bedroom. "Chrissie, you're always so sensible. Island granite, that's you."

"Absolutely," said Christina. "Nothing throws me."

Liar, liar, house on fire.

"But I saved the worst thing for last," said Anya. "First I have to look out the window. Make sure it's not still there." She pushed up the glass and leaned out.

Then she began screaming in horror. Her wails were high and thin like a siren in the distance.

Christina grabbed her, getting a handful of skirt.

Anya ripped free. "Chrissie, your house! It's on fire! Your parents are in it, they're burning up. Oh, my god, we have to save them, come on!"

Anya leaned farther and farther out the window, climbing over the sill, hanging over the cliff.

Christina hung on, fingers laced in Anya's blouse, trying to get a grip on her body. Like the sea captain's bride, Anya tried to go through the glass. "Let go, Chrissie, let go, it's calling me, they need me," Anya screamed.

Christina looked around Anya, trying to see the wet suit, or the cormorant, or the sea captain's bride.

Far out to sea, where they had been born, flames reached into the afternoon sky.

Anya was telling the truth.

My house! thought Christina. I lied, and it did set my house on fire!

Chapter 7

Anya was screaming, screaming, screaming.

Mr. Shevvington was racing up the stairs, Michael and Benj were racing up the stairs, even Mrs. Shevvington was running up the stairs.

Mr. Shevvington got there first.

"Christina!" he shouted. "Christina, stop it!"

Stop it? she thought. Stop trying to save Anya?

"Christina, what are you doing? Shoving Anya out the window?"

Mr. Shevvington jerked Christina by the shoulders, throwing her backward against the wall. Then he hooked his arms around Anya's frail body and pulled her into the room. He rocked her back and forth. "It's all right, Anya, you're safe now, don't be afraid, I've got you."

Michael and Benj burst into the room. Mrs. Shevvington clumped in moments later. Christina was dazed where her head had hit the door jamb. She lay on the floor trying not to cry out with pain.

"What happened?" cried the boys. "Christina, what happened?"

The burning fog. They, living on the island inside the fog, had never seen it. Christina had finally witnessed the apparition that so terrified generations of mainlanders — *Is it a house on fire? A ship in trouble? Are children burning? What shall we do?*

Anya, eyes closed, lashes black against her pale cheek, lay in the pillow of her own hair against Mr. Shevvington. A tiny red rim of Anya's blood decorated the white windowsill like a row of garnet beads.

Voice full of horror, Mr. Shevvington said, "Christina, were you trying to push Anya out the window?"

Michael stood over Christina. From this angle, he was enormous, with feet so large he could step on her, squash her like a bug. She did not recognize him — his folded arms, the underside of his chin, the bagging-out of his jeans at the knees. He was glaring at her.

Christina swallowed a sick dreadful taste in her mouth — a taste of metal, of seawater, of her own blood and bile. *Are they actually accusing me of trying to kill Anya?*

The huffing noise in the room was replaced by the quivering lungs of Michael, Benj, and Mr. Shevvington, by the strange whimpering of Anya.

"No, no, no," said Anya. "Christina would never hurt me — she — I — "

"What then?" said Mr. Shevvington. "Trust me. Tell me. I won't let her hurt you."

But Anya did not seem to remember the fire on Burning Fog Isle, the house she had needed to save, or the "worst thing of all" that she had not yet told Christina. She just mumbled and made no sense.

When Christina tried to tell, the boys said she was yarning, and Mrs. Shevvington said this was beginning to form a pattern, and Mr. Shevvington said he felt the girls should be separated.

"Separated?" said Anya faintly.

"There's another bedroom," said Mr. Shevvington. "We'll move Christina in there. This is not a good situation."

Above them the poster of the sea looked out the window. The fingers that rode the painted white froth beckoned, and the curl of the waves was like the curve of a smile.

It wanted her, thought Christina. The sea wanted Anya. If they separate us, who will keep Anya from the arms of the sea?

But what could she say out loud? Even Michael and Benj seemed to be wondering if Christina really had been pushing Anya! Not Michael, thought Christina, betrayed. Surely Michael knows me better than that!

Mr. Shevvington sat down on Christina's bed. He patted her mother's quilt. It was the flying geese square — tiny, equilateral triangles of calico that flew around and around. Christina made herself think of cloth, needle, and thread; her mother, patiently sewing for Christina, planning something beautiful for Christina. "Sit with me a moment, Christina," said the principal.

Christina did not.

I hit my head, she thought. I have a huge bump

on my head where he threw me against the wall. He *liked* throwing me. And nobody has asked if I am all right.

"You do not know yourself, Christina," Mr. Shevvington informed her, standing up. "I am very worried about you. This kind of emotional disturbance is sad and frightening to us all. We love you, Christina. Everybody in this room loves you. Talk to us about what's bothering you. Do you feel inadequate? Do the mainland children seem much more capable? Are you very, very jealous of Anya?"

Ah, boys. Michael and Benj did not like how the conversation was going. It promised to be full of emotion and blame and they did not want to get involved. They backed out, claiming homework, important re-runs on TV, snacks begging to be eaten.

Mrs. Shevvington smiled.

Anya began brushing her hair. She brushed it with such vigor Christina thought she would pull all her hair out. "I don't want to be by myself," said Anya, looking at Christina and the Shevvingtons only through the mirror.

"I'm only thinking of what's best for both of you," said Mr. Shevvington gently. "You're both denying that anything happened, but the fact is that we walked into a very frightening scene a few minutes ago. I am sure, Anya, that you were not screaming for nothing."

"I told you why she was screaming," said Christina. "She saw the fire on our island and — "

"Christina!" said Mrs. Shevvington. "These stories of yours border on the manic. Call it yarning, or call it criminal defense, I wish to hear no more of it."

"Criminal defense?" repeated Christina.

"Now, now," said the principal to his wife. "We didn't really see. We aren't really sure."

Mrs. Shevvington snorted. With a flick of her fingers she whipped Christina's mother's quilt off the bed and marched into the vacant bedroom beyond the boys' room. "No need to upack drawers," she said. "Michael, Benjamin!" she yelled. "Move Christina's entire bureau into this room."

The boys moved the furniture. Mrs. Shevvington supervised.

Mr. Shevvington began to talk about jealousy and how well he understood it.

Christina interrupted him. She would turn this terrible episode into a little package to be set aside — never opened again — perhaps donated to a church fair. "What's for supper, anyway?"

Michael said from the hall, "Good grief, Chrissie, we run up here thinking you two are being raped or mugged or thrown out the window and all you care about is what's for supper?"

"You know me," said Christina lightly.

But he did not know her. Michael, whom she had loved from birth, was a stranger to her; she was in trouble and he was not with her. Anya was a distant cloud. Benj was merely solid, moving furniture, showing nothing. *Christina was alone.*

It's what I feared most, she thought. I didn't fill

it in on the form but he knew anyway.

They walked down the stairs like a column of soldiers.

Supper was fish chowder, just the way Christina loved it; thick, with milk and butter and diced potatoes. A huge stack of puffy, fresh-from-the-oven baking-powder biscuits sat in a basket lined with a red cloth. Christina slathered hers with honey, and Anya ate hers plain, and the boys put on butter and maple syrup. Everybody had at least two bowls of chowder; Michael crushed crackers into his and Benj slurped his. Dessert was a wonderful cherry pastry from the bakery on the tourist street.

Food is the answer to everything, Christina thought. Especially if it's hot.

Her head no longer ached. Michael's stories about the soccer team he was trying out for were so funny. She planned to go to all his after-school games. She thought about the tape she had to dictate for Dolly. Good thing she had said nothing yet. She really would sound insane talking about posters and wet suits and cruel principals and forms asking if you were afraid.

She thought about her homework. She was eager to get started. She was sure girls like Gretch and Vicki would be perfect at homework; she could be no less.

Christina cleared the table, and Michael and Benj did the dishes. Anya opened her book bag. She looked into her physics lab notebook, with all its blank spaces for her to fill during the year. Anya had gotten an A average in chemistry the year before; no doubt she would do the same in physics. Christina took a little more dessert and nobody objected. Perhaps the Shevvingtons were going to relax the rules a little.

Michael and Benj just sighed. Homework was prison, and the bars had just shut, as they had known would happen, and there was nothing to do now but suffer, do time.

Michael opened to a chapter about comparisons between the Soviet Union and the United States. "*Government*," he muttered. "Who cares about *government*?"

Benj began calculating on Anya's pocket calculator. "Fifty-eight school days," he informed them. "Then I'm sixteen. One and a half marking periods. That's all."

Anya said nothing. She filled in nothing.

Christina opened her book bag. For English they had to write a poem. It made her sick just to think about writing a poem. About having to read it out loud, while Vicki and Gretch and Jonah listened. Smirking. Talking about island girls on welfare.

Mr. Shevvington said, "Christina, you and I will have our talk now. It cannot be postponed any longer."

"What talk?" said Christina.

Mr. Shevvington took her by the shoulder and led her into the library.

His blue blue eyes kept trying to look into her ordinary dark eyes. She found other things to look at. She looked at the empty shelf for a while, and then the pattern in the rug, and next the three dull pencils lying at angles on the lamp table. There were dead bugs lying inside the globe of the ceiling light.

She thought, When did he get blue eyes? He didn't have blue eyes before!

"You're afraid to look at me, Christina Romney."

"I'm not afraid of anything," said Christina.

He said gently, "You didn't fill out that form precisely because you are afraid of *everything*."

The room grew thick and wait-full, like the bedroom upstairs, with the poster of the sea.

"Christina, talk to me about your fears. I'm here to help."

Christina said nothing.

He said, "You want to have no friends? Bad grades? Lonely afternoons?"

His voice softened. It grew thick and sucking like the mud flats. "Then you're doing just the right thing, Christina." The voice caught at her, dragging her down. "It's going to happen, Christina."

It was the dream sequence, being chased, feet stuck, and evil catching up. Christina said, "How can you call this a library when you don't have any books on the shelves?"

"When you try to change the subject like that," said the principal, "I know it is because you are filled with fear. You cannot admit yet that you are a very disturbed child. Christina, it's all right. I understand."

The evening passed.

Michael, Benj, and Anya did their homework at the kitchen table. Mrs. Shevvington prepared her class lessons at the kitchen table with them. Christina sat in the library, waging silent war with Mr. Shevvington.

"I have to do my homework now," she said to him, her final weapon. What principal could argue with that?

"No," said Mr. Shevvington. "I want you to go to bed early, get a solid night's rest, and be able to face the morning with a good heart. I am writing you an excuse to give every teacher."

In his delicate looping hand, he penned:

To whom it may concern:
Christina has suffered a severe emotional distur-
bance, and I have given her permission not to do
homework until she recovers from her distress.
                    Arnold Shevvington
                    Principal

The principal smiled. "Mrs. Shevvington will read this out loud to the class, Christina, so that they will understand why an exception is being made for you."

Christina sucked in her breath. She would rather die than have Gretch and Vicki and Jonah and the rest hear that letter! "I am not distressed," she said, "and I would like to do my homework."

"Now, now," said Mrs. Shevvington. She appeared as quickly, as silently, as before. There was something subhuman about the way she could appear anywhere — like an ant or a mouse, coming through the cracks unheard. "You heard Mr. Shevvington, Chrissie."

But how did *you* hear? thought Christina. Listening at the cracks, as well as arriving by them?

"I think," said Mrs. Shevvington, "the attitude I will take is that you are just very, very tired. You aren't used to the fast pace of mainland life and all those people around you, Chrissie. I think we will give you another chance."

Don't call me Chrissie, thought Christina. Only my very very very best friends may call me Chrissie. And then only sometimes.

"We're going to go on up to bed, now." Mrs. Shevvington took Christina's book bag as if taking custody of a child. She smiled, her teeth round and yellow like a row on a corncob. "With lots of good sleep, we'll behave ever so much better in the morning, won't we, Chrissie?"

Christina stumbled up the stairs.

Each tread caught her foot, and she banged her shins. There was a spider in the shower, and she could not find her favorite nightgown.

She could not imagine morning. Science — where the teacher had said how the island children were always so good! Math — history — what was she going to do?

Christina pulled the quilt over her head, and in the dark nest of her body and the sheets she tried to stay calm. The math was all review; she could do it in ten minutes during homeroom. The social studies she could read instead of having lunch. The science — well, she would just have to wing it. But English — Mrs. Shevvington had assigned them to write a short poem.

Christina hated writing.

Reading was fine; she could read anything and love it. But it did not work in the other direction for Christina.

How Christina loved paper! Fresh, new, first-day-of-school paper. Narrow lines or wide lines, spiral notebooks or three-ringed, arithmetic paper or construction. Blank paper was beautiful with its calm, clean look. But once she touched it messy thumbprints appeared, and violent black slashes where she had meant to cross a T. It wrinkled from the pressure of her clenched hand around the pen, and it tore at the wrinkles by the time she finished.

Blank paper — so nice when she bought it — such agony when she used it.

And writing her own poem?

I need a month just to think of a topic, thought Christina. She thought if she began crying she would never stop; she would be like the tide, and the salt water of her tears would cycle and recycle, endlessly ripping her back and forth.

Anya slipped into the new bedroom. Christina was so glad to see her. The girls hugged and did not let go. It was not like hugging at all, but like leaning. "What happened, anyway?" said Anya.

"I don't know," said Christina. They both knew they were talking about the window, and the burning fog, and the Shevvingtons.

"I couldn't do my homework," said Anya. "I couldn't understand any of it. The pages just sat there looking at me. Christina, I'm going to fail my senior year, I can feel it. And I can't give a speech.

I can't ever give a speech. I can't bear the thought of people staring at me and listening to me and analyzing my words and grading my talk. I'll lose my voice. I'll lose my mind!"

"Hush," said Christina. "You'll be fine."

"Listen to the sea. It sounds like a coffin being dragged over broken glass."

It does, thought Christina. Like the sea captain's bride. And of course there *was* broken glass. She jumped straight through the window.

Anya said, "Sleep in my room. I don't want to be alone in there."

You're not alone in there, thought Christina. The poster of the sea and the huffing are in there with you.

She shivered.

Surely Anya would not try to get out the window again. It had been the illusion of fire — she really had been trying to save the islanders — she had not been trying to jump like the sea captain's bride.

They went into the other bedroom. Anya undressed. She had a lovely body, as white as her face, as untouched by the sun as if Anya had been raised a mushroom. "So what should I do about Blake?" asked Anya.

Christina had forgotten Blake. She had forgotten that anybody but her might have problems. "I don't know."

"I have to see him. I'll die if I don't see him."

She said this with such certainty that Christina thought, Anya *will* die if she doesn't see him. We will all die. That is why we are here. To die. That is why there are no other guests. There must be no witnesses.

Anya put on a nightshirt — a huge man's shirt, with the tails reaching her knees. She was so thin within it, she seemed not to exist from the throat to the knees.

Christina said, "But what was the worst thing? The thing you were going to tell me before you saw the burning fog."

Anya said, "I don't remember. What could be worse than not being able to date Blake?"

Mrs. Shevvington came up to check. She made Christina go back to her room. Alone.

Christina lay in bed listening to the surf, waiting for everybody else to go to sleep. She had a flashlight. *Semper paratis.* Always prepared, that's me, just like the Coast Guard motto says, Christina thought. We island girls are prepared to survive.

Christina slid out of bed and stealthily opened the lid of her trunk, fishing among the sweaters and jeans until her fingers found the thin metal tube. She slid the narrow knob of the torch. The batteries were good. Christina tiptoed into Anya's room and got pencil and paper out of her book bag, since Mrs. Shevvington had confiscated Christina's. She took Anya's chemistry book for a writing surface and tiptoed back to her room. She nearly missed her footing at the top of the stairs and fell down them. In the dark green room Christina curled under the quilt and worked grimly on her poem. Version after version — stupid line after stupid line.

Finally she had something. She got a pen out of Anya's purse and made a final copy.

It was so messy she had to make a second final copy. I'm done, she thought, almost weeping from exhaustion and relief.

She re-read the poem by flashlight.

if I were a sea gull
I wouldn't have to stick around.
if people argued — I would fly off,
swerve, wheel, dip, scream.
a thousand wings of company if I have friends
two strong wings of my own
if I don't.

She liked it.

It was island strong.

Christina folded the good paper carefully and stuck it in her purse. She put Anya's belongings back exactly as she had found them. She didn't stuff the crushed versions in the wastebasket; Mrs. Shevvington might find them and use them for evidence. She stuck them back down in her trunk, under the Icelandic sweater. She slid the flashlight under her pillow. You never knew.

She collapsed in bed, comforting herself with the feel of the seams on her mother's quilt under her fingertips.

The huffing began again.

Christina's heart jolted.

"Fffff," the room said.

It's the tide, she told herself. I already went

through this once today, and it's the tide.

She lay in bed trembling.

"Fffffffff."

Her eyes burned from staring into the dark.

She identified the separate sounds of wind and waves and a distant motor — car, not boat. Her hands tightened around the flashlight, as if she might need it for a weapon, as well as to end the dark.

"Fffffff."

She got out of bed.

The huffing slithered around her nightgown and tumbled through her hair and penetrated her ears like a snake, crawling in, slithering in.

"*Fffffff.*"

It was not the tide. It was in the house.

In the hall a faint light came from the boys' room. Their door was open, their window shades were up. They slept deeply and breathed evenly. The open stairs yawned at Christina's feet and the delicate banisters around the balcony were thin as carved toothpicks.

"*Fffffff.*"

She turned on the flash. Some of the banisters stood straight in front of her, and others grew long and thin, and their shadows fluttered like moths. She swung the flash toward them, and they stood still while the doors to the boys' room and the bathroom vanished. She turned to light those places, and the shadows behind her moved forward and grew fat.

She could not move fast enough. The shadows ate her feet.

The sea captain's house looked down and up at her, exposed in her circle of light; the house all safe in its dark.

"*Fffffff.*"

Christina walked into the jaws of the whispering sound.

It's not the Cove blowing out the candles, she thought, it's here, in this house, somebody having an eternal birthday, never getting the wish right, the candles lighting back up like evil magic tricks.

"*Fffffff.*"

She climbed the open stairs into the cupola.

The stairs were very steep, and had only treads, not risers, so when she flashed the light at her feet, she could see through the stairs, down to the floors below. The shadow of herself was huge, like a flowing Arab robe. She climbed up and up, too many steps, far higher than the ceiling was high, like a cartoon creature climbing beyond the building into the sky.

In the moonlight the cupola glittered. She flicked the flashlight upwards and the glass turned black, reflecting her like a mirror.

She looked up, and left, and down, and right, flashing her torch, searching the shadows. The huffing was screaming at her now, "FFFFFFFF. *FFFFFFFFF. FFFFFFFFF!!!*"

The ghost of the sea captain's bride stood white, frozen by a winter sea, framed by glass, whispering, "*Fffffff. Ffffffff. Fffffffff.*"

Chapter 8

Christina woke up slowly. Her muscles seemed to awaken before her mind, the waking up traveling down her limbs, out her arms to her hands, and finally arriving at her fingers, which hurt; they were cramped.

She opened her eyes.

She was in Anya's bedroom, lying on the bare mattress Mrs. Shevvington had stripped the night before. Anya was in her own bed, covers on the floor in a tangle. Wet salty air filled the room. The girls were holding hands between the beds.

Actually, it was Anya's hand holding Christina's. Her fingers were tight as death.

"Anya?" whispered Christina.

Anya woke up even more slowly than Christina. Her white face was smudged, as if by bruises or oil. The beautiful hair was lank and flat, the eyes dull.

"*Anya?*" whispered Christina again.

"I had the most terrible nightmare," said Anya. She began crying. She made no sound, nor did her eyes or chin quiver; tears spilled like brooks running into the sea. "Chrissie, you needed me. You were fighting the fingers of the dead."

Morning sun lay dazzling upon the sea, breaking through the window glass like a fist.

"What happened?" said Christina. Dimly she remembered the ghost.

"I don't know. The fingers had you, they were pulling you! I stopped them." Anya began shuddering. Her eyes did not seem to see past the iris. She was holding Christina's hand so hard Christina thought the bones might crack.

All memory returned. Christina was disgusted with herself. "That's not what happened, Anya. You were sleepwalking in your nightshirt. You scared me. You went right up the cupola stairs, and you were talking to the tide. You've got to get a grip on yourself." One by one she pried Anya's fingers loose. She tried to joke. "You've got a grip on me right now instead."

When Christina peeled her away, Anya's eyes stayed on her empty hand, and she held the hand up to her face to stare at it, the fingers who no longer had friends.

Christina got off the mattress and walked slowly toward the bedroom windows. There was seaweed on the glass. Forty feet above the cliff. Sixty feet above high tide. And seaweed had appeared on the window?

I won't look down, she told herself. I might see the wet suit. I won't look out, either. I might see the burning fog. I'll just look at the window pane.

And then Christina's fingers iced where Anya had clenched them.

The seaweed was on the *inside* of the window.

Christina lifted her index finger to touch the seaweed. The seaweed was still green and wet.

"Thousands of fishermen have lost their lives in that ocean," said Anya. "And children. And people on vacation. And sailors. And immigrants."

How could it be wet? thought Christina. High tide was hours ago. But even the highest tide of my life wasn't high enough to spray this window with seaweed.

In its time the ocean had yanked down oil rigs and lighthouses, thrown great ships to the bottom, tossed tiny dories onto rocky shoals. So it could hurl a wisp of seaweed in such a way that it landed on the inside of a window.

Anya was drawing dead children and sailors in the air with her hands. "And swallowed the salt water," she said dreamily, "and filled their lungs with ocean, and gagged their final convulsions." She sounded as if she had watched.

"And they're still here," she whispered, getting up, crossing to the window, and leaning way out to stare into the ocean.

"What do you mean, still there?" said Christina sharply. Haven't we said all this before? she thought. How often will we say this now?

Anya smiled madly. "Their shadows still swim. Fight the tide and fling seaweed. How do you think that green seaweed got stuck to the window way up here?"

Christina swallowed. "Uh — the high winds — extra high tides — "

"Don't be foolish. If a wave had touched the top of the house it would have swept away the shutters, it would have been a gale to tear off the town docks."

Christina looked away from the window. Looking at Anya was unbearable. She looked at the poster.

Quiet water. No whitecaps. No shadows beneath the raging sea. Just peaceful blue waves.

It was not the same poster the souvenir woman had thrust into her hands.

"The fingers of the dead put that seaweed there," said Anya. "Sea fingers."

How normal they all were at breakfast.

They had toast today, and bacon and fried eggs. Orange juice in tiny glasses with pineapples printed on them.

Michael talked of soccer practice, and Benj discussed his first project in woodworking.

Not the same poster. How could that be? What could be happening? What power of the sea had made Anya sleepwalk, singing to the tide in the tide's words?

Anya looked down at her plate fairly often, but seemed not to recognize anything on it. She held her fork but did not use it. Mrs. Shevvington said nothing about the rules of sound eating. Christina ate her own breakfast without talking. She stripped the fat off her bacon, which left her with a tiny strip of lean hardly big enough to chew. She ate the toast dry. Perhaps with her allowance she would buy her own jam. Strawberry, the only kind Christina liked. She would hide it between her knees and spread it on her toast while Mrs. Shevvington was pouring herself a second cup of coffee.

I do not believe in fingers of the sea, Christina decided. Anya and I both had nightmares, probably about school. I'm afraid of the seventh grade, and she's afraid of public speaking. It has to be the same poster, I just didn't focus. Today I will be granite again.

Mrs. Shevvington was wearing a cranberry red suit this morning. It was the exact same cut and material as yesterday's royal blue suit. Christina wondered if the woman had a whole rainbow of them — gold and purple and black suits, which would follow one after another, all with the same white blouse. "How are you feeling this morning?" said Mrs. Shevvington to Christina. She bared her corncob teeth.

"I'm very well, thank you," said Christina, peppering her egg.

"And you, Anya?" said Mrs. Shevvington. "How are you?"

Anya was clearly unwell. But Michael and Benj were already filling one of the two sinks with hot water and squirting dishwashing liquid under the flow of the tap. They did not notice that Anya neither heard nor answered the question.

"Any more trouble with the windows?" said Mrs. Shevvington, still smiling.

Trouble with the windows. Anya trying to step through them had been the trouble. Christina had forgotten all about that. Now she remembered Mr. Shevvington implying that she had pushed Anya. It's been one nightmare after another, Christina thought. Pretty soon I won't be able to keep track of them all.

Christina cleared the breakfast table, handing Michael the plates and glasses.

Anya simply stood there, looking disconnected from her own body. Her clothing did not match. She had on an ugly print blouse in faded grey and brown, with a yellow skirt and red shoes. "Did you look in the mirror?" said Christina.

"No," said Anya. "But I looked in the poster."

The fingers in the poster. Were they Anya's fingers of the sea? Had they come to collect?

Had they already collected Anya?

English class was very quiet.

Christina sat behind Vicki and Gretch, and Jonah sat behind her.

One by one, they were forced to walk to the front of the class and read aloud their poems.

Two of the boys could hardly get up there, they were so nervous. The first boy plowed into two student desks and the wastebasket on his way to the front, and whacked his elbow on the blackboard. There is no pain quite so awful as elbow pain; he moaned before starting his poem. "No sound effects, Robbie," said Mrs. Shevvington. "Merely the poem."

The boy had written about the beauty of his mother's smile when he got home every afternoon.

Christina was touched.

Her mother, too, had a welcome-home smile.

Mrs. Shevvington said, "How sweet, Robbie. Immature, however. I am afraid immaturity runs in the family."

Robbie flushed scarlet and tripped going back to his seat.

His mother's smile is ruined for him, thought Christina. Every day this year when he gets home from school and she flings open the door and smiles at him, he'll blush and get mad and avoid her.

She wondered what Mrs. Shevvington had meant about immaturity running in the family, and why she had said such a rude thing.

The second boy rhymed very carefully. To make sure the class followed the meter, he spoke in a singsong. His poem was about summer traffic.

> *Summer traffic*, he recited.
> *Is very graphic.*
> *Too many cars*
> *Really jars.*

He had eight verses like this. Christina loved it. She could see the poem illustrated with fat tourist automobiles and bumper-sticker size lettering.

"Wellllll," said Mrs. Shevvington, adding extra lllll's. She lifted her eyebrows, sharing a joke with the rest of the class. "You tried, Colin."

Christina's smile of enjoyment faded. Colin's head sank between his shoulders like a turtle's. He shuffled to his desk, trying to avoid everybody's eyes.

Vicki was next. Vicki's poem was stupid. It was about the meaning of death as seen in storm clouds. Mrs. Shevvington beamed at Vicki and gave her an A. "Now that," said Mrs. Shevvington, "is a meaty topic. A topic worthy of a poem."

Christina said clearly, "I think a mother's smile is a topic worthy of a hundred poems."

Mrs. Shevvington turned slowly and stared at her. Fyes of mud, skin of jellyfish.

Christina thought, I am granite. I do not flinch.

"Notice how the girl who did not do her homework feels free to make comments," said Mrs. Shevvington.

Christina's heart was hot with pleasure. "I did my homework," she said evenly. "Would you like me to read my poem now?"

The other children were staring at her, in awe, confusion, or amusement.

I have become different, thought Christina.

She had always been different. The one who was painted, the one photographed. But she had not wanted to be different in seventh grade. It was to be the year of being the same! The mainland year, the year of fitting in.

"Do read your masterpiece for us," said Mrs. Shevvington in silken tones.

Christina got up from her desk. Her feet seemed to have gotten heavier; she clumped to the front of the room; when she turned to face the class she saw a haze of unknown mouths and noses, queer staring eyes — strangers, strangers, strangers.

She swallowed.

She unfolded her wrinkled poem.

if I were a sea gull
I wouldn't have to stick around.
if people argued — I would fly off,
swerve, wheel, dip, scream.
a thousand wings of company if I have friends
two strong wings of my own
if I don't.

Jonah Bergeron clapped.

Robbie clapped with him.

The rest waited to see how Mrs. Shevvington reacted. The teacher said nothing about the poem. Instead she walked up to Christina, pushing against her, the cranberry red of her suit shouting as loud as a mouth.

"Why, Christina, you didn't do any homework last night. I myself forbade it. You wrote this poem last year, for some island school assignment. You're handing it in now, pretending you wrote it last night."

"I wrote it under the covers," said Christina, burning. "With my flashlight."

Mrs. Shevvington snorted. "I will give you a zero, Christina Romney. Cheating and lying may be acceptable on your island but they will not do here."

I could push her down Breakneck Hill, thought Christina, and applaud when she got killed.

Gretch and Vicki giggled. She knew they were giggling at her. At her poem. At her zero. At her shame.

After class three things happened.

Mrs. Shevvington said, "You will give me your flashlight at dinner, Christina."

"If you believe I have a flashlight," said Christina, "you believe I wrote that poem using it last night."

Mrs. Shevvington smiled. This time her teeth did not show. It was more a thinning-out of her lips: a challenge. "The flashlight," she said, "is to be given to me."

Why? thought Christina. To cripple me in the dark?

Who is this woman, that she wants to get me? Who am I to her?

"Christina?" said a soft voice.

Christina jumped as if ghost fingers were touching her spine. Then she flushed scarlet. "Hullo, Miss Schuyler," she mumbled.

"Are you all right, Christina?" said Miss Schuyler. Her fat braids lay like a thick honey pillow on the back of her neck. How cozy it must be, to live beneath that hair, thought Christina.

She thought of telling Miss Schuyler about what it was like to live with the Shevvingtons. But she could not do that. Teachers stuck together. Teachers had coffee together and meetings together, and if she told Miss Schuyler, Miss Schuyler would tell Mrs. Shevvington, and somehow Mrs. Shevvington would have more power. "I'm fine, thank you," said Christina, and she skirted around her math teacher and plowed on down the hall, alone.

Power, thought Christina dimly. What is power?

She thought of power plants, and electricity. She thought of nations and wars. Mrs. Shevvington has more power than I do, thought Christina. But what is the power for? Where are we going with it?

Robbie caught up to her, drawing her out of the hall traffic. "Christina? Is that your name?"

She was uncertain of them all now. "Uh-huh," she said cautiously.

How thin Robbie was. How powerless. "I don't want you to get in trouble with Mrs. Shevvington," said Robbie quickly, looking around to be sure nobody heard. "You're new here, Christina. You don't know. *Don't speak up again like that.*"

"But you're new, too," protested Christina. "We're all new. We just started junior high. How can you know Mrs. Shevvington any better than I do?"

Robbie's eyes were old and dark. He said, "I have an older sister." He said no more, giving the sister no name, no description; as if his older sister truly were nothing more than that — not a person, not a soul — just a thing. Christina shivered. Robbie swallowed. Whispering, he added, "She — she had Mrs. Shevvington last year for senior English."

"And?" said Christina.

Robbie shrugged. He walked away. "Just don't talk back," he said over his shoulder.

His sister, then — had she talked back?

But what had happened to his sister? Why did Christina feel that she had just received a gift from Robbie, a present he had been afraid to give her — news about the sister who had no name?

Next it was Blake who stopped Christina in the halls. Blake looked so handsome! Christina wondered if the painters and photographers who came to Burning Fog would want Blake to pose. He did not have an island look, though; she had never seen anybody so thoroughly mainland. "Christina, what happened to Anya?" said Blake. He ran his hands through his thick dark hair and it flopped across his part.

The fingers of the sea, thought Christina. They followed Anya all the way into the school. "I don't know, Blake. What's the matter?"

"She's being weird. She looks funny."

"She's worried about going out with you, and both of you getting into trouble."

"Yeah, I'm worried about that, too. But she was saying — " Blake broke off, embarrassed, because several lowly seventh-graders were listening. "She was saying the sea was gone," he said in a low voice. "She made it sound like the Atlantic Ocean had moved away."

The poster had changed. Could the ocean itself change? If the ocean could change, anything could; none of the laws of earth and life would be safe. If the world were about to collapse, Christina wanted to be on the island with her family, where she knew the rocks and the roses. "I'd better go see," she said. She pushed through the seventh-graders, running out of the building, down the wide steps, between the brick gates, heading for the Singing Bridge.

But it was not Blake running along with her — it was Jonah. Where had he come from? "Christina, you're crazy," he shouted, matching her steps perfectly, so their ankles locked like kids in a three-legged race. "Course the ocean's still there," he said. "If it had disappeared it would have been on the evening news."

"I can't rest easy till I taste it," she shouted to Jonah. "Run faster. We have to get back to class on time."

"Taste?" said Jonah.

"When you take a deep breath of low tide air," said Christina, "you taste it, too."

They reached the Singing Bridge. Cars hummed over it. The tide was high but the Cove was relatively quiet. Waves slapped in a friendly fashion against docked boats.

They stopped, panting.

Jonah said, "Um, Christina?"

The waves flecked a faint mist onto her face. "It's still here," said Christina. She sucked in lungs full of air, salting her mouth and throat.

"There's this dance," said Jonah.

Christina focused on him. She was granite and would not give in to yarns and fancies. A dance. "Oh, we're awful for dances on the island," she said.

Jonah looked relieved. "You're a terrible dancer, you mean? Good, because I've never danced at all. I've hardly even seen dancing except on videos, but

I feel as if I should know how. And this — "

"No, no," said Christina irritably. She grabbed his arm, turning him around, and they began jogging back to school. "*Awful for dances* means we love dances. We have lots of them on the island."

"Oh." Jonah considered this phrase. "Well, will you come with me?"

"Come with you where?"

"The dance."

"What dance?"

"Christina!" he yelled. "The seventh-grade dance! The Getting To Know You Dance! In two weeks."

There had been that form entitled Getting to Know You. There had been that order from Mr. Shevvington that Jonah was to be her friend. She said, "It's bad enough I have to get soup and sandwiches on a blue ticket, Jonah Bergeron. I'm not going to a dance on a blue ticket. Get lost."

Christina walked home with Anya and Blake.

The Jaye boys were not with them. Michael had started soccer practice, and Benj was looking for a job; he said life was too boring with nothing to do but school. He was hoping for a gas station. He liked engines.

Blake said, "Anya, please tell me what's wrong."

She still had her bruised look. Even though Blake clung to her hand, Anya seemed to be alone, lost inside her own body.

Blake pleaded with Anya. He said he loved her. He said he wasn't going to obey his parents; what did they know anyway? He said okay, if Anya wouldn't ride in his car, then he wouldn't either. He would abandon it in the parking lot and walk every step she walked. He just wanted to be with her. Something was wrong, please let him help.

Blake said, "Anya, tell me how you got that big bruise on your leg. And the cuts on your knee." Anya said nothing. Blake lifted the hem of Anya's skirt to show Christina the bruise.

Christina sucked in her breath. "Anya is sleepwalking," she said dubiously, although she did not want anybody to know. It sounded crazy; she was afraid a catalog Maine person like Blake would abandon Anya if she sounded insane. Blake would stick by Anya because he was in the mood to oppose his mother and father; but he wouldn't if everybody else said she was a nut case. Christina stared at the bruise. She could not remember either of them falling, and there had been no crashes among the huffing sounds.

"Listen," whispered Anya. "The sea. It sounds as if it's in chains."

"It's just the tide," said Blake. "It always sounds like that."

"Can't you hear?" Anya cried. "Chains scraping. Ankles caught. Children choking."

"It's the sand," protested Blake. "When the waves go back out, sand is dropped along the way."

Anya shuddered. "It sounds like dead armies marching."

Blake looked at her in despair.

"I will never sleep again," she told him. "You

didn't hear the sea last night. All the dead beneath the waves began breathing again."

Fffffffff, Christina remembered.

"It must have been the wind in the shutters," Blake said.

That night they did their homework at the kitchen table. Anya was writing an essay. "Write about young love," said Christina. "Write about Blake's car."

But Anya was writing about the tide in Candle Cove.

Every twelve hours (plus twenty minutes) the tide licks the barnacles, inching toward the village. Then a queer sickening whisper begins. Ffffff — puffing out a candle. And the entire ocean, laughing because it caught you by surprise, hurls itself into the Cove. You cannot get away. It has you. If you are in Candle Cove, wading, rowing a dinghy, digging for clams, you will die. Candle Cove is the Atlantic Ocean's toy. Like a birthday present, it opens itself every day, hoping, hoping, hoping, to catch you by surprise. And drown you. . . .

Mrs. Shevvington, like the English teacher she was, said, "Anya, two errors here. First, you refer to the sea as if it is a person. As if it thinks and plans. This is called personification. Attributing humanity to things or animals."

"I never said the sea had humanity," said Anya. "The sea is psychotic. The sea is a mass murderer."

"Your second error is pronouns," said Mrs. Shevvington. She was smiling. As if Anya had finally
gotten the lesson right. "The reader cannot tell who
the victim is."

"Me," said Anya. "The sea wants me."

Chapter 9

"Mother?" Christina said, clinging to the telephone. "Oh, Mother, I'm so glad to hear your voice."

There had been a phone line out to Burning Fog Isle all of Christina's life, but not during her parents' childhoods. They had had to use ship to shore radio. Christina blessed the telephone. She just hoped Mrs. Shevvington wouldn't come home and catch her in the forbidden living room before she had a chance to explain everything. "Mother, it's so awful here. I need you," cried Christina. "Please come."

There was a curious pause. It was not like her mother. For a moment Christina thought the connection had been broken, and she imagined the fingers of the sea, taking the underwater cable, tearing it asunder, laughing beneath the waves.

"Christina," said her mother in a queer voice, "the Shevvingtons have talked to us. They were on the telephone with us late last night. Honey, how could you behave like this? How could you forget your upbringing? Rude in school, lying about your homework, frightening Anya, refusing to eat the meals Mrs. Shevvington labors over? Christina, your father and I hardly know what to think."

The black-and-gold peacocks mocked Christina. "Mother, that's not what it's like." The telephone shook in her hand.

Her father got on the extension. She could see them, her mother in the kitchen, fragrant from baking; her father in the bedroom, sweaty from playing tennis. "Christina, when you left the island we were so proud of you, and now look. Cheating and yarning and refusing to obey authority! We don't know what's the matter with you, but luckily you're with people who are used to dealing with difficult adolescents. The Shevvingtons are going to handle it."

"*It!*" cried Christina. "You mean *me*? It isn't like that. The Shevvingtons are cruel people. I think they hate girls. I think they choose a new one each year, and this year it's Anya. The Shevvingtons made us fill out forms about what we're afraid of — acid, or rats! You have to — "

"You're making that up, Christina," her father said. "Christina, honey, no teacher, no principal, would ever hand a form like that to a child."

"No, no. It's true. And this house — I'm sure that the sea captain's bride — or maybe it's the poster, the poster of the sea — "

"Stop it!" shouted her father. "Christina, I won't have this! Mrs. Shevvington told us that you and Anya have some sort of sick game about that poster on your wall. Now you listen to me. When I was a kid, I had a hard time finding my place at the mainland school, too, and so did your mother, and so did everybody else, but we didn't resort to making up ridiculous stories and placing blame on other people, and pretending that the finest, most caring principal the school has ever had is cruel! We just worked harder, Christina. We obeyed the rules! And that's what we expect from you, too."

The phone crackled.

It's the sea listening in, thought Christina. The sea knows what's going on. The sea started it.

Mrs. Shevvington came into the room. She did not look powerful enough to control Christina's parents across the water. But she was. She took the phone, smiling her corncob smile. She told Christina's parents that visits would not be a good idea and phone calls would be worse. There should be no communication between Christina and her parents until Christina had learned to behave.

Christina willed her parents to refuse. Believe in me! she thought.

"Fine," said Mrs. Shevvington. "Arnold and I will keep in touch. The important thing is not to worry." Her smile stretched long and thin and yellow. "We are in complete control of Christina."

Dolly's first tape arrived.

Dolly was bored; it was no fun being the oldest in school; she had to help with the little kids, and this year the kids were really little: five-, six-, and seven-year-olds. Dolly missed Christina. Dolly was sure Christina was having a perfect year. Because that was the only reason Dolly could think of that

Christina wasn't sending tapes — she was too busy and too happy.

Christina had a blank tape. Benj had bought it for her. But what could she say to Dolly?

Dear Dolly, Remember my school daydream? Best friends, laughter, shared snacks, phone calls, compliments, a boyfriend?

I sit alone at lunch. Mrs. Shevvington punishes me for everything. Mr. Shevvington smiles and says I need mental counseling. As for your brothers, Benj won't listen to me; Michael never comes near me; word got around school that I'm weird, and he's afraid it's catching.

I sleep alone in a dark green room that talks to me at night. Mrs. Shevvington took my flashlight, and the light switch for the bedroom is on the far side of the room from my bed, and the light switch for the hall is all the way around the other side of the balcony. I just get under the covers in the dark and hope Anya doesn't jump out her window.

Anya said you can't tell anybody if it's hard; they just worry and they can't do anything anyway. I want everybody on Burning Fog Isle worried about me. But the Shevvingtons took care of that. Nobody's worried. Just mad.

Anya doesn't sleep much any more. She's afraid the seaweed on the window was a sign that the waves are going to come right into the room for her. Her grades are slipping. She breaks down in Public Speaking class and sobs. Mr. Shevvington comes in to give her moral support. She's always thanking

him for being so good to her. He's not good to her!
He's the one who put her in there to start with.
    Mr. Shevvington wrote Anya's parents, Dolly.

    Dear Mr. and Mrs. Rothrock,
    Anya continues to work far below her ca-
    pacity. Just what immaturity causes this,
    I do not seem to be able to find out. Instead
    of growing more mature, contributing more
    in class, acquiring and using skills, Anya
    moves steadily backward. . . .

    I hate Mr. Shevvington, Dolly. You go to junior
high to learn government, begin algebra, increase
your vocabulary, start a foreign language. Me, I'm
learning to hate.
    I cornered Robbie. I asked about his sister. Rob-
bie was afraid, but he told me in the end. Val was
sweet and friendly once. Sang in the choir, won
prizes in the art fair.
    "Ordinary," Robbie told me. "But nice." He
frowned; this was the real stumbling block. Val had
been nice. . . . She became nothing. It wasn't that
she stopped being nice. She stopped being anything.
    Val slipped during her senior year; forgot to do
homework, stopped washing her hair, avoided her
friends, ate strange things, like Spaghetti-O's cold
from a can. She adopted a single outfit — torn cor-
duroy pants and an old shirt of her father's — and
wore it daily for weeks. She was not on drugs, Dolly.
She was not on booze.
    She's locked up now. The Shevvingtons recom-

mended a really good adolescent mental hospital.

Jonah has fallen in love with me. I know. I wanted to have a boy fall in love with me. But I wanted to choose what boy. Jonah is overflowing with emotions that I do not share. I have to ask for instructions. "How do you feel now?" he asks. I say to him, "How should I feel?" He loves to hear me talk about the island, and whenever I finish my stories he laughs. I can't tell if he's laughing at me or with me. I want to be friends with the real kids! Like Vicki and Gretch. But they don't pay any attention to me. Except when they're laughing at me.

Oh, Dolly, it's so awful. The only good thing is you are safe on Burning Fog. I know you hate sixth. I hated it last year, too. But sixth grade is safe.

Sometimes when Anya wakes up at night, and slips into bed with me, her feet cold, her hands cold, and she says that the fingers of the dead are walking on her back —

We hang onto each other, Dolly, but I can't hold on forever. One of us is going to fall.

Well, of course she couldn't send a tape like that to Dolly.

So she sent nothing.

"I have to give a speech about the ocean," said Anya, twitching with nerves. They were up in Anya's bedroom, Anya staring into the poster of the sea, Blake and Christina staring into Anya. In the afternoon Blake was always at the Schooner Inne now. The Shevvingtons stayed late at the high school, Michael had soccer practice, and Benj had a job pumping gas at the Mobil station.

"Who says it has to be about the ocean?" demanded Christina. "Talk about the sky, or the grocery store, or Blake's catalog clothes."

Blake was sprawled on the floor of Anya's room. Christina was never afraid when Blake was there. She did not know what it was about Blake that kept away the fingers of the sea. Was it that he was a boy? That he was in love? That it was daylight?

"Mr. Shevvington says I have to overcome my fears. He says I have to tackle the scariest topics of all." Anya whispered to the poster. "He knows all my fears."

If I had those forms, thought Christina, if I showed them to my mother and father, then they would believe! Then they would realize that Mr. Shevvington is the one who is sick, not me.

She wondered where the forms were kept. Who else had read them? Who else had had to fill them out? What about Val's forms? What had Val been afraid of? How had Mr. Shevvington destroyed Val?

Anya ran her fingers through her hair and pulled it down over her face to hide herself. Blake sighed and pulled Anya off her bed and down on top of him, putting her hands and hair away from her face. "Anya, stop being so worried. It's only a high school class. The worst thing that can happen is that you'll forget your speech and have to sit down."

Anya burst into tears. She quivered when anybody raised a voice around her now. Mr. Shevvington never raised his voice, so she skipped a lot of her classes and huddled near his desk. "Blake, don't yell at me. I can't date a person who yells at me."

"I'm not yelling at you!" yelled Blake.

"Anyway," said Anya, "Benj is not afraid of anything. If I have a job, I won't be afraid, either. So I'm quitting school, too. I found a wonderful job. Where the water is all locked up."

"What?" shouted Blake. "Quit school? Are you out of your mind? You *will* end up a wharf rat then."

Christina had thought romance would be fast red cars, billowing black hair, long drives down the coast, alone together, kissing, and in love. That's what Blake thinks, too, she realized, watching him watch Anya. But Anya — the most romantic-looking person in Maine — Anya doesn't even know.

Blake changed subjects. Perhaps he thought he could change Anya as easily. "I made you a present," said Blake pleadingly. "It's a calendar. Full of our dates. Nothing but our dates."

He had drawn the squares and the months himself. Each week was illustrated with cartoons cut from the newspaper — *Far Side, Funky Winkerbean, Peanuts, Cathy, Garfield* — cartoons about love and romance and boys and girls. Each Friday and Saturday listed a movie, a drive, or a dance that Blake would take Anya to.

"That's so romantic!" said Christina, hugging herself.

"A paper calendar?" muttered Anya. She never talked in a normal voice any more; she just whispered to herself or to the sea. "Silly little squares with numbers on them. The only true calendar is the tide. It speaks to you; it ordains the time."

"Anya," said Christina nervously, "when the tide speaks to you, don't answer."

Blake got up off the floor. Christina could feel his rage. No, no, Blake, don't leave her! Don't break up! You're all she has. I don't count. I'm just the seventh-grader in the other bedroom! She needs you!

But Blake was trembling; his muscles quivered strangely, and she could not tell if he wanted to hit something or hug somebody.

"I'm putting an end to this," said Blake. He slammed the window down, hard enough to break the glass. He yanked the paper shade so it snapped on the roller like a gunshot and jerked the thin cotton curtains closed.

"You can't get rid of the sea that easily," said Anya dreamily.

"Anya, I don't know what's happened to you. But it makes me nervous. And my parents — listen, the screwy way you talked in front of them this afternoon — Anya, it didn't help us any. *What is going on?*"

Anya turned very slowly, like a ballerina. She arched onto her toes and with a long, slow wave of her own, pointed to the poster of the sea. "Ask it," she said. "It knows."

How big he is, thought Christina. She was filled with admiration for him, for his body and muscles and anger.

Blake attacked.

For one horrible minute she thought she would witness a homicide after all, that Blake would kill Anya with his bare hands. His fingers were huge and curled, like the souvenir woman's, like Mrs. Shevvington's, like the waves on the poster of the sea.

Blake ripped the poster off the wall. Sliding his fingers under the paper, he tore it off in great strips and chunks. The sound filled the room, like the huffing of night, the sound of mutilating. He threw the strips of poster behind him. Bits of green ocean and blue wave fell in the four corners of the room.

Anya jumped onto her bed, getting off the floor, as if the bits of poster were rats about to bite her bare feet. "I didn't do it," she cried. "It wasn't me!"

"Who are you talking to, Anya?" shouted Blake, shredding the poster. "This thing was printed by the thousands in some factory in Boston. It's nothing. *Nothing*. See? I tore it up. It's gone."

Why didn't I think of that? wondered Christina. I could have torn it up myself. How clever Blake is.

The bedroom door was flung open, hitting the wall. The last strip of torn poster hung on the handle like a Christmas tree decoration.

"What is going on here?" Mrs. Shevvington said in a tight thin voice. "Anya, what are you doing, bringing young men up to your bedroom? Christina, why are you in this room? You have your own room, as I recall. Blake Lathem, I thought better of you. Since you have been associating with these island girls, your behavior has become worse and worse.

I plan to address your parents about this. They have been discussing the idea of boarding school with Mr. Shevvington, to remove you from Anya's influence, and I see that they were very probably right."

Anya cried out, draping herself over the bed like some old damp towel. Blake went white.

"Nothing has happened," said Christina. "Nothing was going to happen. We were just watching the tide." She hated how people yielded to Mrs. Shevvington. Why didn't they kick her in the shins? Why didn't Blake, who had enough rage in him to break windows, attack her?

"Oh, you were, were you?" Mrs. Shevvington smiled. It was a brighter, more challenging smile than any she had directed at Christina before.

War, thought Christina. We're at war now.

"Anya, Blake, go downstairs immediately. Christina, clean up the mess in this room."

They were gone, Mrs. Shevvington pushing Blake and Anya downstairs like a high wind shifting driftwood.

Christina was alone with the shreds of poster. From the bathroom she got the whisk broom and dustpan. She began sweeping up the bits of paper.

Ffffffffffff, began the house.

She brushed.

Ffffffffffff, said the house.

Ffffffffff, said the walls and the floor and the glass.

Christina tried to stand up but there was weight on her, as if she were standing under water.

If I can just get downstairs . . . she thought.

With the others. With Blake and Benj. I know it's just the tide. I know it funnels sounds up through the foundations and between the cracks and inside the cupola windows. I know it's just Candle Cove.

She dropped the whisk and dustpan in the hall. She grabbed the banister. She could not remember the way to the stairs. "I'm granite," she whispered, "it's Anya who is the tern." She felt herself tip, as if her granite was only a facade, and indoors, inside her rib cage, under her skin, she was as weak and scared as Anya.

She heard the ocean clapping with delight. It's the waves against the rocks, she told herself.

She smelled the sweat of the sea. It's just the salt spray, she told herself.

She fell, clinging to the rope, eyes squeezed shut against the salt water, praying for help.

"Christina," said Michael, laughing. "You look so funny hanging onto the banister like that. You know we're not supposed to run down these stairs. They're too steep." He helped her up. He said, "I've heard dumb rumors about you in seventh grade, Chrissie. You've got to shape up. What's the matter with you? Don't you want to fit in? You're giving island kids a bad name. You of all people!"

Chapter 10

In English class Mrs. Shevvington was doing adjectives. She would call upon a student, give him a noun — like "prairie" or "ocean liner" — and he would have to think up ten adjectives. Mrs. Shevvington had a stopwatch and they went fast, like a spelling bee. It was fun. Christina hoped she got a good word.

"Burning Fog Isle," said Mrs. Shevvington to Christina.

She made a face. That was no challenge. "Rockbound," she began, counting on her fingers, "salty, windy, isolated, pink, lonely, foggy, beloved, famous, and popular."

"Very nice, Christina," said Mrs. Shevvington. "Eleven seconds. Quickest of all so far. No hesitation. But why 'pink'?"

"The granite is pink. The pink flecks are called 'horses.' My grandmother was called a horse in the granite and so am I."

"A horse in the granite," repeated Mrs. Shevvington. "What does that mean?"

"Tough," said Christina. "Impossible to break."

She met Mrs. Shevvington's eyes, but there was nothing to meet. The woman was simply an English teacher working on adjectives. Today when I am strong enough to meet the enemy, thought Christina, there is not one.

"Do you have electricity out there on that island of yours?" said Gretch scornfully.

"Oh, we have all the amenities," Christina told her. "Hot water, telephone, television, microwave oven, the works." She ached for friendship. Who wanted telephones when you couldn't talk to your mother? What good were hot showers or the evening news when you needed love?

Mrs. Shevvington said that Burning Fog Isle had quite an interesting history. The class looked as if they found that hard to believe. "History," said Gretch, "is never interesting."

Mrs. Shevvington smiled. "Burning Fog has always been crime ridden."

The class laughed. Christina was enraged. How dare anybody say bad things about her island? "We are not crime ridden," she said furiously. "I don't think there's been so much as a wallet stolen in my whole life."

Mrs. Shevvington beckoned to the class, and everybody leaned forward, following the call of that powerful finger. "Before the Revolutionary War, the people on the island were simple fishermen or farmers," said Mrs. Shevvington with contempt. "Mostly they raised sheep," she added, as if sheep were invented to be laughed at.

The mainland kids giggled. They looked at Christina with pity.

"Before the Revolution, the islanders were very religious, very stern. After the Revolution, the only religion on the island was rum. Islanders were drunk all the time." Gretch and Vicki snickered. Mrs. Shevvington not only allowed this, but joined in. Mockingly, folding her arms across her chest, she faced Christina. "Burning Fog boys ceased to be sea captains," she went on, "and became pirates." The class laughed out loud. "This may sound quaint — an attractive little myth — but bad people populated Burning Fog. Vicious, amoral people. In fact . . . *murderers*." Mrs. Shevvington savored the word. The children mirrored her, whispering the word to each other, letting it murmur like a distant motor. "Generation after generation the people of Burning Fog salvaged from ships they wrecked themselves."

"We did not!" cried Christina. "You're making that up."

Mrs. Shevvington raised her eyebrows. "No, Christina, I read it just last night in a book about the shoreline." She lifted the local Historical Society's privately printed book and proceeded to read aloud. The names of the supposed shipwreckers were Romney and Rothrock — her family and Anya's. "You, Christina," said Mrs. Shevvington, "come from a long line of murderers."

The fingers of the sea pressed into the small of Christina's back.

She remembered Anya stepping out the window toward Burning Fog.

She thought of Mr. Shevvington implying that she, Christina Romney, had been trying to push Anya out.

They are going to murder Anya, thought Christina. They are going to blame it on me. They are going to say that I come from a long line of murderers. That my great grandparents thought nothing of enticing ships onto shoals.

"Christina the Criminal," said Gretch, giggling. "I like that."

"Christina the Pirate's Daughter," suggested Vicki.

"No, that's too romantic," said Gretch.

The class laughed.

She went through the cafeteria line. She filled her tray. She passed in her blue ticket. She could feel them all watching her. She could feel them all waiting, getting ready to mock or laugh or sneer.

I will not break down, she thought.

She walked alone, threading through the filled tables. She did not attempt to say hello and she did not look to see if anybody would let her in. She knew that Gretch and Vicki controlled popularity and they had decided she could not have it after all. Christina walked steadily to one of the empty tables and pulled out a chair. It scraped a little on the floor, the sound her soul would have made if it could have cried out. The seventh grade smirked and turned its back.

It seemed that all the girls came in pairs and trios and quartets, and giggled together, shared candy bars, alternated arithmetic problems on homework. She wanted to sob, or throw herself at their feet, begging to be allowed to giggle with them.

Every time she reminded herself that she was granite, it seemed to be a little less true. They were chipping away at her.

Jonah sat down with her.

She hated him for it. No boy sat with girls. Not in seventh. It was better to be alone than have a boy take pity on her.

"I'm not here because of Mr. Shevvington's orders," said Jonah. "I really and truly want to go to the dance with you."

Christina made a foul noise.

Jonah said, "You're beautiful, Christina. You really are."

"Get lost, Jonah Bergeron."

"My middle name is also a graveyard name," said Jonah. "It's Gideon. Jonah Gideon Bergeron."

"So?"

"So don't you think you could go to a dance with Jonah Gideon?"

"What makes Jonah Gideon an improvement over Jonah?"

"He's more interesting," said Jonah. "More depth."

Christina snorted. Her mind was occupied with

other things. She wanted the flashlight. Her allowance was like nothing. One snack, one ticket, a single item at the pharmacy, and it was gone. If she needed a piece of posterboard for a school project, or Magic Markers, or more gym socks — there it went. "Jonah, would you loan me some money?"

"How much?"

"I don't know. I need a flashlight and batteries."

"What for?" said Jonah.

Christina studied him.

She saw nothing new. Jonah was incomprehensible. Why would he keep asking her to that dance when she was so mean to him? Was he a pipeline to Mr. Shevvington? If she said things to Jonah, would the Shevvingtons be told, line by line, betrayal by betrayal?

Jonah Gideon Bergeron, of graveyard names.

Was that what it meant to be friends with Christina Romney? Graveyards?

Christina took a risk. "The Shevvingtons are trying to hurt Anya and me. I need a flashlight because we're isolated up there on the third floor in the dark and we're not safe." She stared at him, her eyes hot. Her own mother and father had not believed her. Her own mother and father had listened to half an argument and cut her off. Why would Jonah believe?

"I believe it," said Jonah slowly.

Christina's hair prickled, silver and gold.

Jonah wet his lips. He leaned toward her, his eyes darting like minnows in shallow water. "The Shevvingtons — there's something about them,

135

Christina. Nobody knows what it is. The parents think they're perfect, but — well, like, there was Robbie's older sister. And everyone thinks that Anya is next."

Christina felt herself grow lighter, as if she might float on fear. "Next what?" she breathed. "What is the end of it? Where are the Shevvingtons taking us?"

Jonah shook his head. "I don't know. Nobody knows. Robbie's sister just disappeared."

"You mean, like *murdered*?"

"No, no, she's there. Her body is there. She's just not — nobody knows, Christina. She doesn't have a personality anymore. It's like the Shevvingtons took it away, and now his sister is nothing. Vacant. Only the bones, but no soul."

Christina thought, What is a flashlight compared to the power of the Shevvingtons?

"Listen, Christina, tell somebody. You have to have help."

"Like who?" Christina was perilously close to crying, right here in the school cafeteria, with Gretch and Vicki watching. How they would love to tell Mrs. Shevvington that they had made her cry. "Did anybody help Robbie's sister? Has anybody offered to help Anya?"

"They don't see," said Jonah. "Only the kids see, and they don't do anything. They watch, though. They're like jungle animals. They watch the predator take the weak."

Christina felt Gretch and Vicki watching.

"But maybe a teacher . . ." Jonah's voice petered

out. He knew no teacher would take a side against the principal. They'd never believe anything awful about Mr. Shevvington. All grown-ups thought he was so wonderful, so kind — caring — careful — and that disgusting phrase all grown-ups adored, *such a good role model.*

"Miss Schuyler? In math? She's not too bad," said Jonah.

If my own parents don't believe me, thought Christina, if Michael and Benj don't believe me, why would Miss Schuyler?

And yet, and yet . . . only Miss Schuyler had ever asked if Christina was all right.

Jonah said, "I'll get you the flashlight." They were not Jonah's eyes looking out of his face anymore, but the eyes of somebody older and tireder. Had he aged, thinking about her danger?

After school she met Blake and Anya. She was their chaperone now, their stage manager.

Anya began whistling, face puckered up as if her lips were stuck in a Coke bottle. She whistled no melody, but a steady note, like the wind playing cello through the ropes of a high-masted ship.

"Stop it," said Christina.

Islanders never whistled. Whistling called up a wind. But you don't want a wind, it's Weather; nobody wants Weather.

"We're going for a walk," said Blake firmly.

That's what it is to be almost eighteen, thought Christina, full of awe. I can *say* I'm granite, but a person like Blake really *is* granite.

Blake took Anya's arm in his right arm, and Christina's in his left.

"Talk," said Blake. "I want to know. I know you're not crazy. Tell me what's wrong."

"I quit high school today," said Anya. "I'll show you where I'm working. You can visit me there if you like."

"Quit high school?" echoed Blake. "Mr. Shevvington let you? But Anya, you're first in the class! You're going on to medical school someday, remember? Remember your dreams?"

But Anya's dreams were no longer of school. Christina knew her dreams; dreams of the bottom of the sea. What kind of job? she thought. It will kill Anya's parents if she's really quit! She is the light of their lives.

And her own parents. What would they say? Would they blame Christina? And Michael and Benj, whom she hardly knew, and they were only three weeks into school — it was still September — still autumn. The longest month, she thought, in the history of the world.

Down Breakneck Hill they went together, feet sideways to keep from falling. By the bottom, gravity was making them run. Blake held the girls' arms to keep them with him.

Christina fell in love with Blake.

It happened in an instant, and she was no longer their escort, their advisor, their little sister. She loved him.

Oh, no, no, a thousand times no! thought Christina. He's Anya's! Anya loves him, he loves Anya and he's old, old, old. I'm only thirteen, and Blake is eighteen, it's impossible.

His arm linked in hers was heaven.

His scent was of men and wool jackets.

His shoulders were higher than hers. Wind blew Christina's tri-colored hair over his jacket. Ribbons of silver and gold danced over his shoulder and then blew gently onto his face. Blake smiled down at her. A ribbon of her own hair made a mustache over his lip.

Kiss me! thought Christina.

She tried to kill the prayer — for it was Anya he should kiss. Anya with whom he must have his romance.

But she looked at his lips anyway and dreamed.

She could have walked forever, hanging onto his arm, dreaming of him, pretending Anya was not on the other side.

"Here," said Anya happily. Her voice was warm and cuddly.

Blake let go of Christina's arm. "Anya, this is a laundromat."

Anya's bright smile was like gauze over her face, a bandage over her craziness. "See how safe the water is!" she told him. "It's trapped behind little glass doors. All the waves in here are under control." She spread her arms to embrace the laundromat.

Dreary people sat mindlessly staring at the clothing through the little glass doors of the washers and dryers. Lint lay on the floor and a few abandoned socks were pushed in a corner. A tired woman with seven baskets of laundry was struggling to fold sheets by herself.

Blake controlled himself. "Anya, you're an honor student. Like me. You're going to college. Like me. You're going to be a doctor."

"Folding," Anya nodded, hearing nothing he said. "It's clean and neat. You can keep track of things here."

Blake dragged them out of the laundromat. The humid, linty air stayed inside the building, along with the dirty linoleum and the broken change machine. It seemed to Christina he was crying, but that was impossible. People like Blake — men like Blake — did not cry in laundromats.

He's crying for Anya, she thought. He knows she's gone. She's already in the washing machines. The Shevvingtons, or the poster of the sea took her. Anya knew all summer they were coming for her. It was just a matter of time.

Christina did not know where they were going. Blake no longer held onto her; he needed both his arms for Anya. "Talk, Christina," he ordered her. "Anya can't."

Christina nodded. She flicked the switch on her cassette recorder. Benj had bought her blank tapes; it was time to use them. She would record it for Dolly at the same time. Then there would be two who knew. She began with the strange glassy weather the day they were given the poster of the sea. Anya said nothing, but nodded and nodded, as repetitively and as meaninglessly as the waves of the ocean. Christina finished with Michael catching her on the stairs.

Blake said, "The poster is just a poster. Maybe there is more than one. Maybe Michael or Benj thinks it's funny to put up new ones, or substitute different ones."

Christina knew they had not. Their lives were not interlocked with hers and Anya's; you could not tell that Michael and Benj occupied the same house. In some strange way, the Shevvingtons had housed them on the same floor, fed them at the same table, and yet they were not together.

"And the tide is just the tide," Blake said. "All this puffing of candles is famous. People visit this town just to hear that. That's why Schooner Inne will probably succeed — people who want to wake up in the middle of the night to the sound of Candle Cove. The house has the same foundation as the cove — the same rocks, Chrissie. You live in that building and you feel the same slap of the wave, the same cannon of sound. There's a pattern, but I can't see it. I'm going to, though, Christina."

A pattern, she thought. Like my mother's quilt: flying geese or feathered star pattern. This is an evil pattern. Not cloth, but paper and sound. But who? Only people make patterns? But who cuts this one, and why?

Anya said, "I feel the tide coming. I know because my fingers are on fire." She held out her hands. Long, slim, white fingers without polish, without rings. Christina took one of Anya's hands and rubbed it. "There," she said. "Does that put the fire out?"

Christina heard the hum of cars on the Singing Bridge. The more we talked of the sea, she thought, the closer we had to get to it.

Standing on the dock that summer people used for their yachts and power boats and cabin cruisers was the brown wet suit.

Beckoning.

"Blake," Christina breathed, tugging at his arm and pointing. "There it is. The brown wet suit."

Blake saw. He let go of Anya and began running. "I'll get him!" he screamed back at the girls. "Then we'll have answers!"

A storm had come up. It had not yet burst, but the air was full of electricity and salt wind. Black clouds against a pink-and-gold sunset swept in from the sea, fighting to see who got rain, who got thunder, who lightning.

The wet suit left the narrow gray painted dock. It ran lightly up and over the cliff opposite the Cove from Schooner Inne. It ran to one of the rickety ladders that led to the mud flats below. It began the descent into the cove.

Blake ran after it.

The wind came up, stronger than before, and the black clouds closed in. Christina shouted after Blake, but he didn't hear her.

"I could watch the waves forever," said Anya dreamily. "What I do is pick out one and follow it all the way in. Look, look!" she cried. "Look at the one I picked out. It's running away, breaking against the rocks, trying to get to safety."

Christina gasped.

The tide was coming in. The wet suit was going right into it. Blake was following right after him.

"Blake!" she screamed. "Blake!" She turned to Anya, pushing her onto a tourist bench flanked by yellow chrysanthemums. "Stay here, Anya."

"No," said Anya sadly, "the wave didn't make it. When my time comes to run, I will break against the stones, too."

"Anya!" screamed Christina. "Shut up. Be sensible. Just sit here!" She turned and ran after Blake, screaming his name, screaming for other people to help. But there were no other people. How could a town whose livelihood came from the sea, from these wharfs, from the tourists who usually sat there painting and photographing and absorbing local color — how could it be empty?

The storm gathered above Christina, so low in the sky she felt she could throw a basketball into it and break the clouds. It prickled with electricity. She could feel the lightning coming. "Blake! The tide is coming in! Don't go down the ladder!"

Christina did not know how she could have run so fast, over the outcroppings, over the crevices and cracks, to reach the top of the ladder.

But she was not fast enough.

Blake was halfway down. He turned to see, not Christina, but the water: a tidal wave, larger even than normal because of the storm. A great green blanket, eager to smother him, and carry him to the mattress below where he would sleep forever.

He seemed frozen on the ladder.

Instead of racing up to Christina and safety, he clung to the wood and stared at his death.

The tide slammed into Candle Cove like cannons going to war. It attacked the rocks and crashed against the crags. Its whitecaps reached like fingers to take Blake.

"Blake, Blake, Blake!" screamed Christina, reaching down. The water was so high it drenched her.

Blake looked up at her. The last thing she saw of Blake was his fear: the terrible knowledge of his fate written on his face as clear as print.

Chapter 11

"The poster," said Christina for the third time, "was torn into pieces. Blake ripped it off the wall. Now it's together again. That's why Anya dropped out of high school. That's why she's working in the laundromat."

Christina's father jammed his hands into his jeans pockets and stared out the window. Christina's mother began crying quietly.

Mr. Shevvington said, "Thirteen is a vulnerable age. There is often borderline behavior. I think we can be grateful that your daughter is not into drugs or alcohol. I think her personality can be saved." He paused. "I'm trying to think of a way to phrase this gently. But there is no gentle way. Island life is very isolating. Ingrown. Naive and unsophisticated. When a young emotional girl, full of hormones, full of dreams, finds herself facing reality for the first time, with classmates who are better prepared, more in touch with the times, better dressed, and so forth, it isn't surprising that there's a collapse."

Christina's mother had buried her face in the crook of her elbow. Christina's father had now turned his back completely. Mrs. Shevvington was smiling. Neither of the Romneys saw it. Mr. Shevvington's soothing, serene voice droned on and on. How much he was able to bring into it! Drugs, violence, "the times in which we live," "teenagers today," even the entire twentieth century.

Christina interrupted him, for which her parents scolded her. She said, "I have thought about it and thought about it. The only people who could have put up a new poster are the Shevvingtons. And they could have put a bit of seaweed on the inside of the window, and they could have told Anya story after story about the sea captain's wife stepping through the cupola and they could have — "

She stopped. She was frozen like a Stone Tag statute by the look on her parents' faces. "Do you seriously believe," said her father, through gritted teeth, "that a high school principal is going to do silly, childish things like switch posters in the middle of the night in order to frighten a vulnerable seventeen-year-old girl?"

Christina stared at him. That was exactly what she believed. She had said it over and over now. Why weren't they listening to her? She could make the facts no clearer.

"I feel so guilty!" Christina's mother burst out. "I thought we were doing so well by our daughter!"

"And you tried," said Mr. Shevvington sympathetically. "I believe that all parents do the best they can. Unfortunately, as in situations like this, the best is sometimes not enough."

Mrs. Shevvington had set the table in the Oriental dining room, amid the golden peacocks and the black gardens. She served a wonderful meal. She had a standing rib roast, with a delicious, smooth, dark brown gravy, and oven-gold potatoes. She had yellow squash, green beans, and brown bread and, even if you didn't like vegetables, the table was colorful and smelled delicious and looked thankful, like November, like harvest, like love.

The room gave off an aura of love, the way only a feast and a family can do, and only Christina knew it was false. Her parents thought it was kind and thoughful, full of effort and preparation.

"Mr. Romney," said the Shevvingtons gently. "Mrs. Romney." They sounded as if they were addressing an election crowd. "Although we do not wish to jump to conclusions, it looks as if Christina has always been very jealous of Anya. They were unable to share a room and had to be separated. Soon after that Christina even felt she had to take away Anya's boyfriend. Now it would be nice to think that Christina just flirted, but evidence is that Christina tempted Blake to show off. To save a life, supposedly. Some man in a wet suit that nobody else saw."

"Blake saw him," said Christina. She felt like a piece of wood. They could have nailed her to the front of a sailing vessel now and used her for a figurehead, and she would last through any weather. She felt varnished and she thought, That souvenir woman with the leathery skin. Anya said if she touched her she would turn to leather. I've turned.

"Blake," Mrs. Shevvington reminded them all, "was whisked away to boarding school the moment he could be taken out of the hospital. According to Blake's poor parents, the boy hardly knew what he was talking about."

"He knew," said Christina. She could not bear thinking of Blake and yet she could think of little else. He seemed to be beside her, talking to her, touching her. The Shevvingtons were right about one thing — she had had a crush on Blake. A crush that began as they ran down Breakneck Hill and lasted only that short, terrifying afternoon. Blake had been badly bruised, his shoulder dislocated when the summer person — some birder with binoculars — had jerked him to safety. Christina had not been allowed to see him. Anya had not been allowed to see him. When they telephoned the Lathems, Blake's parents hung up on them. "Don't harrass us," they said. They told the Shevvingtons (or at least the Shevvingtons said so) that those two island girls were such a terrible influence and so dangerous that they had to move their son immediately. And they did.

Move him where? Christina thought constantly. Where is he living? What school is he going to? Does he think about us? Is he worried about Anya? Does he remember he was chasing the brown wet suit?

Or does he truly, actually, think that I talked him into a suicidal run down the cove ladder?

Oh, how she yearned to see him! She thought of him so often and yet sometimes she could not quite remember his features; the more she thought of him the more his face eluded her.

Blake's scrape with death had been too much for Anya. The fingers of the sea had truly grabbed him. Christina was unable to convince Anya that the fingers of a real person — a birder walking by — had rescued him. That real people won! And so could Anya, if she got tough with her fears.

There was no toughness in her.

She had quit high school. She was working at the laundromat. Her parents had come to talk to the Shevvingtons. The Shevvingtons had very graciously agreed to keep Anya with them even though she was no longer going to public school and not rightly an island boarder. Perhaps she needs a year off, said the Shevvingtons sympathetically to Anya's horrified, heartsick parents. Every morning now when she left for the laundromat, in her ill-fitting jeans and unmatched blouse and sagging sweater they said to her, "This is good for you, this is right for you."

And Anya believed them.

Christina, remembering what Robbie had said, looked very hard into Anya's soul. She was not sure there was one left. Anya was empty, like an old Coke bottle in the recycling pile. The Shevvingtons were recycling her, all right. But into what?

Christina had made Robbie come to the laundromat to look at Anya. "Yes," Robbie had said, "that's just like my sister. Nothing left."

"Do your parents blame the Shevvingtons?" asked Christina.

"Of course not," Robbie had said bitterly. "They think the Shevvingtons are the ones who helped her last as long as she did. They think the Shevvingtons are kind and understanding."

All parents are alike then, thought Christina, looking at hers. They are actually grateful to the Shevvingtons! My own mother and father are probably going to end this dinner by thanking them!

Mr. Shevvington continued. "Christina knew better than anybody when the tide would come in; Christina is obsessed by that tide and by Candle Cove. She even pretends there is a tide right in her bedroom," said Mr. Shevvington sadly. "Brought us a piece of seaweed she claimed landed on that window sixty feet above the highwater mark." Mr. Shevvington paused. He had a wonderful sense of timing, Christina would grant him that. He said to her parents, "Christina knew Blake would reach that ladder just as the tide thundered in."

Nobody talked about that terrible sentence. It just lay there, implying terrible things.

Christina said to her parents, "*Listen* to me! Listen to *me*!"

But it never occurred to Christina's parents that the Shevvingtons might lie. The Shevvingtons were Authority, they were The Principal, and The Teacher, and The Innkeeper. They told The Truth.

They Knew Things, they had Experience, they were Understanding and Caring.

Her mother, weeping, said, "We have spent thirteen years listening to you, Christina. I guess we made a lot of poor choices. Now it's time to listen to the people in charge of you."

Her parents went back to the island. Without her. They cried, and they hugged her, and they promised to write and send her presents and they begged her to "shape up" and they said they loved her . . . but they left.

Christina thought, some people on islands *are* naive and innocent. Not me — but my own parents. There is evil in this house, and they didn't feel it. It took Anya, as it took Val, and now they're going to try to take me. Well, they won't. I am granite.

In English Mrs. Shevvington discussed a poem by Carl Sandburg. It was very short.

Christina did not consider it a poem. It was called "The Fog." She made a face at it.

"Christina?" said Mrs. Shevvington. "You have a thought to contribute?"

They waged war unceasingly now. The class knew it was war, and had divided into teams. Gretch and Vicki of course joined Mrs. Shevvington, bringing along with them every other girl in the class. The boys just loved a fight, any fight, and goaded Christina continually.

Christina thought she might not actually be the loneliest person on earth, but it certainly felt like it. She had had Dolly for a best friend all her life.

To have nobody, nobody at all — and yet rows of girls sitting inches away from her! — it was the worst thing on earth.

"Fog comes like wall to wall carpet, suffocating the view," said Christina, who had known more fog, more intimately, than any of them. She remembered vividly the day when she was five, out with her parents, suddenly caught at sea in a fog so thick they couldn't see each other, let alone navigate. Her parents began story-telling to keep their little girl calm; that was the day she learned about their courtship, how they saved money to buy their first couch, how her grandmother had given them the family's only wonderful antique, the Janetta clock.

But she said none of this. Anything she said would be used as a weapon against her.

"Time for our weekly extemporaneous essay, class. Put all books beneath the desks or on the floor. Take a fresh sheet of paper and a pencil." The class obeyed with the speed that always followed Mrs. Shevvington's requests, as if they were infantrymen saluting. Mrs. Shevvington got out her stopwatch. "Ready?" she said.

"Ready," they chorused, although none of them were. They hated spontaneous writing. Mrs. Shevvington had scheduled it every Friday until kids starting getting sick on Fridays just to miss it. Now she would spring the essay any time.

The topics were chosen to upset Christina; she could tell by the smirk on Mrs. Shevvington's face.

The fourth week in September — the morning after Blake — Mrs. Shevvington had said, smiling at Christina, "Two page essay. *How Will It Feel to Die?*"

The whole class looked at Christina — had not Mrs. Shevvington foretold what would happen? Had not their respected teacher told them how Christina was descended from murderers?

The following week, which was the first week in October — "One page essay. *Noises in the Night.*"

Now it was the second week in October. The children shivered, knowing the topic would be scary. Sometimes Christina thought they liked it — it was kind of like participating in a horror movie.

"What if," said Mrs. Shevvington, pausing suspensefully, "what if your parents . . . . decided . . . to abandon you?"

The class shuddered in delicious fear.

But what was Christina to write? Because her parents *had* abandoned her!

One parent of one child — only one — had come in to argue about the choice of writing topics. The parent left convinced that Mrs. Shevvington was a very *creative* teacher, with *meaningful* topics that made children *think* and *produce*. Now the parent went around town telling people what a *splendid* teacher Mrs. Shevvington was.

Sick, thought Christina. The Shevvingtons are sick. She looked at the blank piece of paper in front of her. What to write about? She had to pass in a paper or her failure to cooperate would be one more thing to tell her parents. She ignored Mrs. Shevvington's topic and titled her essay, "What is it like to live on an island?" It was important to write something that could be shared with the class, because Mrs. Shevvington always picked Christina's paper to read aloud.

She wrote, "Anything that happens on an island is important. A broken plank on the town dock, a large mail delivery to the Swansons, a litter of kittens at the Rothrocks, a new rope on the tire swing at the school. Everybody knows, and everybody cares."

The timer went off. Mrs. Shevvington picked up the papers with her sick, gloating smirk. Then she did an unusual thing: she read and corrected each paper on the spot. "Why, Brandi," she said, "I like this sentence. 'If my parents deserted me, I would collapse.' Now I want you to add two more sentences of description to that. How would you collapse? Describe your body and your mind in a state of collapse." She handed the paper back to Brandi. Her eyes were bright, hoping, perhaps that Brandi would collapse right then and there.

Brandi, however, had broken the point on her pencil and could think of nothing to add and the mood was not conveyed to her.

"Why, Christina," said Mrs. Shevvington, frowning over what Christina had written. "Having trouble?"

"Why, no," said Christina. "Whatever made you think that, Mrs. Shevvington?"

The rest of the class sat up in anticipation.

Not one child had ever told their parents about this war. Not one ever would. It was just something that happened in seventh grade — one person got picked on, and at least Christina could give back as much as she got. Besides, she was different anyway; she was from the island and probably expected to be picked on.

"A great big reader like you, Christina, ought to enjoy writing as well," said the teacher.

Christina thought this was ridiculous. Why should somebody who liked reading books also like writing papers? That was like saying somebody who liked watching basketball should also like playing it. What if you were three feet tall and crippled? Which was how Christina felt when she had to write something down.

The door to the classroom opened.

The class turned as one to look.

It was the eyes you saw first: eyes like drowned Peg's — blue husky dog eyes. Eyes like a doll's, rotating mindlessly in the sockets. It was the clothing you saw second — leathery, heavy stuff, like armor. And third — third — you saw the hands. Hands that were twin to Mrs. Shevvington's. Hands that curled and beckoned like a hawk's talons. Heavy with rings, shining stones that sparkled, the fingers laced across the chest, ten spikes looking for something to stake.

"Ah, yes, Miss Frisch," said Mrs. Shevvington, her s's hissing like snakes or sea water. "Christina? This is your mental health counselor. Misssssss Frisssssssch."

They had brought the counselor right into the classroom.

Right in front of Vicki and Gretch and Robbie and Jonah.

"Christina?" said Mrs. Shevvington. Today she was wearing an emerald green suit. The green was a splat in front of the chalkboard. "I am so sorry you will be missing the rest of English class. Vicki will bring you your assignment. Vicki, she will be in the nurse's office."

"Oh, dear," said Vicki. "Are you sick, Christina?"

Christina sat locked to her chair. It was the souvenir creature, or her sister. I can't get up, she thought. I can't go anywhere with that.

The class was staring at her. Their eyes were wide, accusing holes, saying, *Are you sick? Crazy sick, demented sick, deranged sick?*

"Why, Christina," said Mrs. Shevvington. "I seem to recall you saying one day that you were a horse in the granite." She laughed. "Island children have such quaint sayings. Come, Christina. Be a horse in the granite for us."

She managed to slide out from under the desktop and straighten up.

No seventh-graders spoke.

They just watched.

And smiled.

Christina wet her lips. She tried to find her books on the floor beneath her seat, but they seemed too far away to reach. Her hands were too chilled to move and would not close around the edges of the texts.

Robbie got out of his seat to retrieve the books for her. The class giggled and became seventh-graders again, teasing cruelly in loud, high voices. "Robbie likes Christina, Robbie likes Christina, nanny nanny boo boo."

Robbie whispered, "Christina, that's the one they sent my sister to. *Be careful.*"

Chapter 12

Christina walked beside the thing. They moved past the other seventh-grade rooms and into the stairwell. Christina stayed on the landing, holding onto the heavy fire doors.

"Christina?" said Miss Frisch.

"I don't feel like talking," said Christina. She forced herself to look into the blue eyes.

"But we have so much ground to cover," said Miss Frisch. Anya had been right: Those were Peg's eyes. Husky dog eyes.

"Did you have the souvenir shop on Burning Fog?" asked Christina.

The creature's face changed expression. It seemed to be laughing. "Run a souvenir shop?" it repeated, amused. "On an island?"

"Are you the tourist who threw a hot dog to Peg, so Peg would go overboard and drown?" said Christina.

A body pressed up against her from behind. A flat hand in the center of the spine. It pushed lightly. Her heart screamed, her soul turned to ice; it was going to push her into the blue eyes, push her into the dead —

She turned to face it.

She would never let it get her from behind.

It was Mr. Shevvington.

But he did not speak to Christina. He was too busy smiling. "Did you get that taped, Miss Frisch?"

"Yes, of course."

"The parents will be most interested to hear those insane statements," said Mr. Shevvington. "Now Christina, let's all go downstairs together and talk for a while about your problems."

She was only thirteen. She was only five feet two inches tall. She weighed only ninety-four pounds. She was a little girl. Their shoulders were wide, their bodies tall, their strides long.

Mr. Shevvington's hand closed around her left wrist, and Miss Frisch's talons closed around her upper right arm, and they walked her down the stairs like a prisoner or a prize.

Christina thought, Somebody be with me! Please. Somebody. Mother, Daddy, Anya, Jonah, Blake, somebody!

But nobody came.

There was nobody to come.

Nobody believed in her.

Mr. Shevvington said, "You have destroyed your parents' love for you, Christina. Love is a fragile thing. You broke that love."

"They still love me," she said. "I know they do."

"Then why aren't they with you?" said Mr. Shevvington.

"Because you made them go!" she cried.

Mr. Shevvington frowned. "Christina, what parent would abandon a little girl just because somebody says so? Your parents have given you to us. Because you killed their love by being such a bad girl."

Down the stairs they went, through the doors, out into the hall near the cafeteria. The cafeteria was empty, chairs stacked on tables for the janitors to mop. The school was silent, as if every class had been dismissed or were taking final exams behind closed doors.

Mr. Shevvington was happy. Miss Frisch was smiling.

This is how they talked to Val. To Anya. And Val and Anya believed. Well, I don't believe. I will never believe. And I won't go into the nurse's office either, thought Christina. She said loudly. "What are you doing to try to get Anya back in school, Mr. Shevvington?"

"Unfortunately getting back into school is not easy," said Mr. Shevvington. "A girl nearly eighteen who leaves of her own free will. . . . We can't just re-enroll her."

"If Anya had the flu, she'd be out for a week and you'd let her back. If I can get her to — "

"You," said Mr. Shevvington, "are going nowhere near Anya. I've seen what happens when you and Anya are together, with your jealousy and your violence."

She lost control. "I am not violent!" shrieked Christina, hitting him with her book bag.

Miss Frisch dictated into her cassette, "The patient punctuated her statement that she is not violent by hitting the principal with all her strength."

Christina began laughing hysterically. Hysteria had never happened to her before, nor had she ever witnessed it. The laughs that bubbled out of her were creepy and frightening. She wanted to stop herself, to cut the laugh away, like the crusts off bread, but the laughter continued. Miss Frisch held her cassette right up to Christina's face, like an oxygen mask, and dictated over the sound of the crazy laughter. "The patient laughed at Anya's predicament."

Past the art room.

Past ninth-grade history.

Past the foreign language labs.

That must be where the fear forms are, thought Christina. In the nurse's office. They'll make me fill out one of those forms and then they'll know what I'm afraid of, and they'll attack, just the way they did with Val and with Anya.

I must not go into the nurse's office!

They passed the first set of auditorium doors and the row of pay phones in the lobby.

They passed Miss Schuyler's room. Christina's math teacher sat alone, correcting papers. She waved at Christina.

Mr. Shevvington coughed, politely putting a hand up to cover his mouth. The hand that had gripped Christina's arm. She was half free. She considered biting Miss Frisch to make her let go the other arm, but the thought of that creature's leathery skin against her tongue, inside the privacy of her mouth, was too terrible. She stomped on Miss Frisch's foot instead.

Miss Frisch cried out, wincing — and let go.

Christina ran into Miss Schuyler's room.

"Why, Christina," said Miss Schuyler. "You're here early. But never mind. I have it all ready. Good morning, Mr. Shevvington. Good morning, Miss Frisch. How nice of you to bring Christina for her tutoring." She smiled at them sweetly. "You need not stay. Christina and I will be fine."

Fine? Christina ached from fear. Her knees hurt, and her spine seemed fractured. It was hard to stand, impossible to walk. Miss Schuyler kicked a chair beneath her and she collapsed on it.

"Decimals," she said. "Quite simple, really, Christina. Begin on page forty-four of this workbook."

Miss Frisch said, "Christina is scheduled to have mental health counseling this period, Miss Schuyler."

Miss Schuyler laughed incredulously. "I could believe Christina would teach a class in mental health, but she certainly requires no personal assistance, Miss Frisch."

Christina held onto the workbook. Was there more than one war going on in this school? Was Miss Schuyler at war with Miss Frisch?

"Christina has been having a difficult time lately," said Mr. Shevvington, turning his serene, convincing gaze upon Miss Schuyler.

But nothing happened. Miss Schuyler was not convinced. She merely raised her eyebrows and touched her old-fashioned, honey-colored braids. Christina wondered how long the braids were. So thick that Miss Schuyler could be Rapunzel, and let them dangle out of a tower window. Miss Schuyler said, "Really, Arnold. I hope you have not been listening to rumor. That is the mark of a poor administrator." She turned away from him and said, "Christina, dear, page forty-four, please."

Christina could not even read the page numbers she was so nervous, but she flipped some pages and took the pencil Miss Schuyler handed her.

Mr. Shevvington and Miss Frisch left the room.

Christina said, "How did you know? Why did you save me?" Tears lay inside her eyes, and her chin and her knees were shivering, like separate leaves on a tree.

Miss Schuyler said, "You looked desperate, my dear. I thought I would give you a few moments to compose yourself. Now tell me what upset you, Christina."

Christina told everything. Not because she was sure of Miss Schuyler, but because it was time to tell. Time to let go and bring in an ally.

Time to surrender? thought Christina, half aware that Miss Schuyler could be another one. One of THEM. Am I falling into their hands? she thought. Is it a trick, like multiple posters?

But it was too late. She had told all.

There was not much time. Another math class would soon fill the room. No doubt Mr. Shevvington or Miss Frisch would be there waiting in the hall to catch her.

Miss Schuyler frowned. "Christina, that is quite a tale."

Christina felt herself turning to nothing, following in Val's and Anya's footsteps. It was a pitiful feeling. Not like a balloon being popped — sharply, with a pin, but oozing, air seeping out invisible leaks until there was nothing left of the balloon but an empty piece of color on the ground.

There would soon be nothing left of Anya. Anya would not even have color. She dressed in nothing but black and white now. Like a photograph of herself.

Miss Schuyler said, "I think I will get in touch with Blake first. A nice young boy. He's at Dexter Academy, as I recall. Now do not be afraid of the principal or that counselor. They have no supernatural powers, Christina. Nobody does. They have managed to upset you so much that you are imagining things. The wet suit is simply some out-of-season kook in a wet suit and the poster is merely a poster." Miss Schuyler frowned slightly, tapping her pretty cheek with her pencil. Christina had not previously thought Miss Schuyler a pretty woman. Perhaps the person who rescued you was always beautiful.

"However it is quite clear to a newcomer in the school, such as myself," said Miss Schuyler, "that there is some association between the Shevvingtons and Miss Frisch." Miss Schuyler pushed the pencil into the honey braids and left it there, like a miniature six-sided yellow sword. "Something unhealthy," said Miss Schuyler. Her pretty frown grew heavier, until it took over her entire face, aging her first one decade, and then another. "Possibly even, something cruel. But why?" She took Christina's face between her two hands, and held, it, as if Christina had more to tell.

"Val and Anya," said Christina, " were sweet and innocent. And — and they're doing one each year. Maybe they did girls in other towns. Maybe — Miss Schuyler, where did they come from, the Shevvingtons? What have they left behind? Are they teachers because — " Christina could hardly say it, because Miss Schuyler was a teacher, a wonderful teacher. "Are they teachers because every year there are new ones? New innocent girls they can rob of their souls?"

Because what fun would it be to destroy somebody nasty and mean? Christina thought. You would not enjoy destroying Gretch or Vicki. You would have the most fun ruining the nicest people.

Miss Schuyler took the workbook out of Christina's hands. Christina had not written a single number down, or even a single decimal.

"Christina," said the teacher dryly, "I am convinced that our principal is not a nice man. But I find it hard to believe he has an actual program he executes in town after town, destroying the souls of innocent victims."

I lost her, thought Christina. Grown-ups can only tolerate half the truth. I went too far, telling her all. Next time I tell anything, I must tell only little easy pieces of it. But then who will bother to help me?

Christina tried to stay granite. She tried to find the bright side. I have half an ally, she told herself. She half believes me.

Miss Schuyler seemed to look so far away she might have had a view all the way to Burning Fog Isle.

Christina thought, But Anya's parents and mine are quite literally at sea. How safe, how delightful for the Shevvingtons! They will take each of us from Burning Fog. They will take away our souls. "What can you do, Miss Schuyler?" said Christina, her hands knotted like the nets of lobster traps.

"I can do nothing. They have convinced the entire school system of their kindness, their understanding, their perfection. But I will watch them, Christina, and I will be your protector. So do not worry." Her eighth-grade class began coming in. Very gently Miss Schuyler added, "And don't magnify it either, Christina. It's not so dreadful as you're making it out to be. It's not nice. But it isn't deathly, either." She drew the pencil out of her hair, like a conductor closing off the chorus, and turned to her class.

Christina left numbly.

Out in the hall hundreds of teenagers knew exactly where they were going, and whether they had their homework done, and which book to carry. Christina knew nothing. Her head swirled. Her brain must look like her mother's marble cake — chocolate and white spiraled together as the wooden spoon drew through the batter. She felt loose and unconnected.

Out of the chaos emerged Mr. Shevvington. He connected to her wrist again. Firmly. "Come into my office."

"I don't feel well," she said. "I need to lie down." Miss Schuyler is wrong, she thought. It goes way beyond what she saw. *The Shevvingtons are evil.* And nobody knows but me.

Mr. Shevvington smiled. "That's fine," he said. "The nurse's office is just where we want to be."

Vicki and Gretch, arm in arm, stopped in the hall to watch them. "Why, Mr. Shevvington," they said, "is she still sick? Poor, poor Christina."

Mr. Shevvington said, "I think perhaps you girls have been hard on little Christina." He made her sound like a pitiful, stupid thing that people tried not to sit next to because of the smell. "Christina needs help, you know, and popular, pretty girls like you, Vicki, and you, Gretchen, could help her."

Vicki and Gretch tossed their hair like synchronized swimmers and preened in the hallway.

Remarkable, thought Christina. He can sound like Mr. Understanding, Mr. Deep-concern-for-troubled-girls, and yet he's made it infinitely worse. On purpose.

"A little bit of attention from girls who know how to behave properly," Mr. Shevvington continued, "would be the making of Christina."

Christina's loose, cake-batter brain became a loose, cake-batter stomach. It roiled and turned inside her like Candle Cove with the coming tide.

"We're pretty busy," said Vicki.

Gretch nodded.

Mr. Shevvington was very sympathetic. "Of course you are," he said. "You're the kind of girls who will be class leaders and team captains. I'm not suggesting that you adopt her as a cause and give up homework for her!" He laughed warmly. "Just a few minutes here and there."

Like taking a dog for a walk, thought Christina.

Vicki said, "Well, I suppose after school, maybe we — um — " Vicki tried to think of something she could fit Christina into.

Christina threw up.

It was wonderful. Disgusting, hot slime came up out of her stomach, burning her throat and mouth, and hurling itself on Gretch's designer jeans and Vicki's beautiful university logo sweatshirt. It dripped crudely down their chests and onto their pretty shoes.

Gretch screamed. Vicki clawed at herself. Christina said, "I need help. Please? Since you're so popular?"

Mr. Shevvington wrote out late passes for Vicki and Gretch. They went sobbing to the bathroom. Christina he hauled down to the nurse's office. What a weapon, thought Christina. She said to him, "I feel very unsettled. I may throw up again."

Miss Frisch was apparently not free this period. Mr. Shevvington told her to clean herself up and lie on the white cot in the corner behind the screen, and he would be back shortly. Christina drank from the water fountain until the horrible taste was out of her mouth, but she didn't have to clean her own clothing up; she had missed herself.

It's all in the timing, she thought, proud of herself.

And then she thought, *I'm in the nurse's office.* I am sure the fear files are here.

She looked around the room. White walls with posters on dental hygiene and sexually transmitted diseases. A large sink with jars of cotton wads, Q-tips, and tongue depressors. An arsenal of aspirin and some witch hazel.

Christina began flinging open doors. Behind the counter doors were rolls of paper towels, bandages, Kleenex. In the wall cabinets lay every size of Band-Aid known to man.

She whirled to go through the desks. Only one drawer was deep enough for file folders. It did not open immediately. Christina played with the pencil drawer until whatever catch attached to the file drawer loosened up, and she could ease it open.

She flipped through the tabs of the file folders. Statistics. Racial characteristics of the school system. Measles and inoculation data. No good.

She shut that drawer and went to the other desk. Reports on diseases, conditions, symptoms, and cures. Come on, come on, Christina thought, where are your student-by-student files?

She scanned the room.

There was a computer screen on the counter in the corner.

She turned it on, pawed through the little plastic

box of diskettes, and read the labels. They were individual files, all right, but the master disk was not among them. Christina turned to the nearest desk and began rifling through the shallower drawers.

There was a sharp explosive flash behind her. Miss Frisch had photographed Christina going through the desk drawers.

Chapter 13

All it takes is one rainstorm, thought Christina Romney. The lovely scarlet-and-gold autumn leaves are torn from the trees and the foliage season is gone: Bare branches and a dark horizon are all that's left.

She kicked her way through a pile of leaves, turning her socks gray with leaf dust, even though the leaves were gold. There was a chill in the air distinct from previous nights. It was winter-cold, not autumn-cold.

"Supposed to be a hurricane coming," said Michael joyfully. Michael loved fierce weather. Benj told him not to talk about it, not even to think about it.

Benj thinks the weather can hear us talk, thought Christina.

It was island thinking. Island superstition. A year ago Anya had thought no differently; now she had moved beyond superstition; she thought the house and the sea could hear her, too.

"Hurricane's down by Maryland and Delaware

now," said Michael, "but it might swing north."

"No," said Benj. "It's going inland. Stop your noise, Michael."

If I were home on the island, my mother would go on a winter hunt, thought Christina.

A winter hunt turns up matches for mittens, boots that fit, and the grocery bag that the long winter underwear was put in the year before.

Christina ached for her mother. She yearned for her father. But when they had come in on their own boat for an emergency meeting with the Shevvingtons — and with Miss Frisch — about Christina's thievery, when they had seen the Polaroid shot of Christina with her hand literally in the drawer where the petty cash was kept . . . they collapsed weeping. This time Mr. Shevvington did not have to recommend anything at all; they begged him. They said, "Please control her for us, please teach her better than we were able to, please take her!"

Christina marveled that it was so easy for the Shevvingtons.

Michael and Benj were going back to the island for the weekend, and they were going to try to talk Anya into accompanying them. They walked toward the laundromat.

"Bet we'll be stranded," said Michael hopefully. "High winds, gale force, can't come back to school for weeks."

Benj laughed. "Bad weather is always over by Monday morning, Michael. Don't worry, you won't even miss first period."

Michael was saddened. He said, "But maybe the

Shevvingtons' house will come down in the hurricane. I don't know how it's lasted so long on that cliff anyway. It's in a very vulnerable position."

"Don't say that," ordered Benj. "Christina has to stay there during the storm." Benj made a face. "Not that there will be a storm," he corrected himself.

She thought about Burning Fog Isle. She had experienced many severe storms, but none with a wind so strong that houses were thrown about like too small lobsters tossed overboard. Would her mother and father be all right?

She was finding it difficult to remember her parents' faces, or Dolly's laugh. She had made the mistake of saying that at breakfast and of course Mr. Shevvington heard and said, "Christina, this is serious personality disintegration. You have not cooperated with me on seeing a mental health counselor."

Michael and Benj went on eating cornflakes.

Mr. Shevvington put an arm around Christina as if they liked each other.

But he does like me, thought Christina suddenly. He likes what he can do to me.

They were at very close range. She could see now that he wore contact lenses. He *could* change the color of his eyes! So that was how his eyes darkened and grew bluer. How could she have been afraid of his eyes? They weren't even real.

"Boys," said Mr. Shevvington, "take this letter to Anya's poor parents. It isn't much in the way of comfort but at least they'll know we did our best by their poor daughter. We always thought she would become a wharf rat and now she has."

"You did not think that!" cried Christina. "You thought she would have an honor roll year, and be the star of the senior class, and — "

"Christina," said Mr. Shevvington, "stop yarning. Michael, Benj, have a good visit on the island. Say hello to your parents for us."

Miss Schuyler is on my side, Christina consoled herself. You can do anything if you have somebody on your side. She looked at her tormentors, who were both smiling, unpunctured by Christina's or Miss Schuyler's scorn.

Mrs. Shevvington's yellow teeth lay in her mouth like seeds waiting for winter birds to eat them. The teeth smiled, as if they too were thinking of eating.

Christina shuddered.

She stuck to the boys. The boys thought nothing of it.

The laundromat was stupifyingly hot and humid.

It was another whole world in there: linty and gasping and wet. Anya was even thinner, which hardly seemed possible, and even more beautiful, which was surely not possible.

She was wearing, because of the heat, a thin white cotton gauze dress with white lace around the throat. She had caught her black hair in a thin white ribbon and the bow lay against her cheek like a white rose. Her hair in the humidity of the laundromat had puffed like cumulus clouds.

"Jeepers, Anya," said Michael, "you look like a bride."

"I am," said Anya.

The boys stared at her.

At least this time they noticed something wrong, thought Christina grimly.

"Whose bride?" said Benj warily. "Blake's not around any more, they got rid of him."

"The sea," said Anya. "Nuns marry God. I will wed the sea." She folded a hot pink T-shirt, neatly turning the short sleeves in to the center and tucking the bottom up. She turned the shirt over, admired the flawless folding, and added it to a pile of somebody else's clean clothes.

Anya, who had been first in her class, future doctor, Blake's girl.

"Listen, Anya," said Benj, "come home for the weekend with us. It'll do you good to see your mom and dad. Frankie's boat leaves in half an hour. Everybody on the island is worried, Anya. Come on. Please?"

Anya shook her head. "I have work to do." She brought out a pen-and-ink drawing she was working on. At first it looked like waves from Japan or China, arching sea foam with hooks. But when you looked closely it was a hundred hands, a thousand fingers, all reaching for the same thing: Anya.

"I'll do the laundry for you," Christina offered. "I can't go home. My parents don't want me."

"They would if you'd behave," Benj told her. "Michael and I have about had it, Christina. I suppose you didn't really do anything wrong, but it looks wrong, and it makes the island look wrong, and it's time you stop and think before you do stupid, dumb things that hurt everybody else."

"What kind of friends are you?" she cried, stomping her foot. The sound was oddly drowned in the sogginess of the room. Anya added several more fingers to her curling waves. "Why don't you believe me? Why would you believe the Shevvingtons?"

"Mr. Shevvington is the principal," protested Benj. "He's not going to lie. Anyway, they caught you. They have the photograph."

"I wasn't taking money. I was looking for the files with those papers we had to fill out."

Benj shrugged.

Anya whistled mindlessly. Two notes, back and forth, back and forth. "Don't," said Benj. "You're whistling up a wind, and a wind right now means weather and we don't want weather. Hear?"

Anya gave no sign of hearing anything. She held up her own hands and studied them like a manicurist. "I can't figure out whose hands they are," she said.

Is there another town full of vacant, stunned girls, whose souls were sucked away? thought Christina. A town the Shevvingtons finished with and got tired of?

"Come with us, Anya. Okay?" Benj and Michael Jaye were uncomfortable. They didn't want to be in this ugly, damp place, with its mildewed walls and the madness that wafted off Anya like a breeze.

Christina wondered if the Shevvingtons were tired of Anya. If they had finished with her yet. If they don't have Anya to toy with, she thought, they'll need another girl. And the only one around . . . is me.

"We had boiled dinner last night," Anya said. She frowned. "Corned beef, cabbage, potatoes, and turnips. I hate boiled dinner. It makes me feel old and crippled and penniless."

The alternative to getting old is dying young, thought Christina. What have the Shevvingtons been saying to her?

"Mom's having a fish fry," said Michael. "We haven't had decent fish since we left the island. Come on, Anya. Chrissie'll fold your shirts."

But Anya just kept folding, smiling at the T-shirts as if she were tucking tissues in her trousseau.

Christina, Michael, and Benj sat on the dock, feet dangling toward the water. A stiff, biting wind blew in from the Atlantic but in the sun the boards were warmish. They felt splintery and familiar. Bird-lovers who visited Burning Fog Isle every autumn to witness migrations, binoculars and cameras hanging around their necks, waited with the children for Frankie's boat. Out on the rocks, seals sunned themselves and cormorants spread their wings to dry. They looked like dirty shirts hanging on the clothesline.

Christina thought of the island as heaven, a place of autumn colors and Thanksgiving coming. But she was not there, and she could not go there, and sometimes she wondered if it even existed.

Autumn was Christina's favorite season. She loved fall: the carving of pumpkins, the early dark of afternoons, the cutting out of construction paper turkeys for Thanksgiving.

All these seemed a distant memory, something that grandmothers told their grandchildren about and nobody quite believed.

She made herself think of the letter Frankie would bring from her parents. The tape from Dolly.

If she knew Dolly, it would be a good tape, full of gossip and laughs.

"I just like to sit around aggravatin' people," Dolly liked to say. (That was what her grandmother liked to say, actually, and Dolly had just copied. But she was right. The trait had skipped a generation. They were both excellent at "aggravatin' " people.)

Dolly, as far as Christina knew, was ignorant of what had happened at Schooner Inne and school. Mr. and Mrs. Romney were silenced by shame and Michael and Benj by confused loyalties. As for the tape she had recorded when she was talking to Blake, it had vanished. Anya had been holding it, but by the time the ambulance came and Blake was taken away and the police had questioned Christina about the wet suit, Anya no longer had the cassette recorder in her hands and could not remember ever having it.

Frankie's boat nosed into the harbor. Rindge barked a greeting. Frankie tossed Christina a line, which she whipped around the cleat on the dock. Frankie unloaded the boat, saying good-bye to passengers who thought he was an exotic, exciting sea captain, posing for tourist photographs and helping nervous day trippers who were afraid they would fall between the boat and the dock.

Then he handed her something better than a letter: her mother's own baked beans.

Christina's mother put sliced onions, salt pork, brown sugar, and molasses into the beans, adding a little salt and dry mustard and a pinch of ginger. Her beans were wonderfully moist. Even people who didn't like beans loved Christina's mother's beans. Baked bean suppers had raised money for repairing the island fire engine and adding to the tiny school playground. Christina had loved that, but Anya used to yearn for a city, where they would raise money with art auctions and opening-night theater tickets.

And now Anya just wanted to fold other people's shirts.

Christina held the casserole in her two hands and warmed herself on her mother's love. She's not so mad at me after all, thought Christina. She baked me a dinner.

Benj was roughhousing with Rindge. Frankie was saying to a birder, "Course, it's exactly a century now since the last big one. So you can kinda feel it coming."

"Feel what coming?" said Christina.

Frankie shook his head. "Ocean gets tired of lying there, I reckon. Every fifty, every hundred years, she's got to kick up. Been fifty years since the hurricane that ripped down half the North Woods, tore the summer people's houses off the island. Figure we're due."

Christina shivered.

"Yep," said Frankie, looking out to sea at perfectly ordinary waves, "I think I see a swell. Beginnings of our own hurricane." Frankie sounded happy about this, as if, like Michael, he had been yearning for his very own hurricane. "Got to get back to the island and batten down," he said. "Got to close up shutters, tie down everything that moves, lay in a supply of bottled water and canned hash."

"That sounds like fun," said Michael. "Bottled water and canned hash. Gosh, Frankie, can I come live with you during the hurricane?"

"Yeah," said Benj, "at least lay in a supply of chocolate chip cookies, Frankie."

Frankie kicked the boys on board. He chewed on his pipe stem, looking Christina over from top to bottom. He knows, thought Christina, hot with shame. They know on the island; somebody talked; somebody said that Anya went crazy and Christina turned to crime. Do they all believe it? Do they all think I'm bad?

"You want to come, honey?" said Frankie. His eyes were full of affection. She wanted to kiss his weathered face a hundred times; somebody out there still loved her.

More than anything on earth she wanted to come with him. But she was not wanted. She shook her head, the barest movement, trying not to cry. "Say hi to my parents," she whispered.

Frankie grinned at her. "You're a tough kid, Chrissie. Now you lissena me. Don't let them get you down. I went to school on the mainland once, too. Hurricanes are easier." He rumpled her hair.

He was right; hurricanes had to be easier. But it was not school she was fighting. Why were all grown-ups so sure that if she only "adjusted to school," everything would be perfect? She could adjust for a hundred years and the Shevvingtons would still be evil. "I don't know if I'm that tough," said Christina.

He chewed on his pipe. "What you need is sumpin' to hang onto when the wind is bad. Take my baseball cap." He put his old red-and-white cap on her head with the bill backwards and yanked it down over her eyes. "Bye, kid."

She watched Frankie's boat until there was nothing left to watch, only a silver gleam on a satin sea.

The sea whispered to her, soft as a caress, lapping her ankles like a kitten. *I am your friend. Come to me. You'll be safe with me.*

"Never!" cried Christina Romney, straight into the wind. "And you can't make me, either! I am a horse in the granite! I am of the island and you will never win!"

The wind argued, flinging her words back into her mouth again. It tugged at Frankie's baseball cap until she had to hold it on with one hand. She pressed the baked bean casserole into her ribs and toted it on her hip.

The wind attacked.

Flags stood straight out, painted against the cruel sky, and people on sidewalks tilted their bodies to fight the force of the wind. Children laughed. Dead leaves went berserk.

Christina staggered up Breakneck Hill. The wind pulled her back down. Out at sea she could see the boats scudding at great speeds. Speeds that would be fun if you were Michael and not so much fun if you had a long way to go before you found a safe harbor.

Christina had no safe harbor.

The only place she could go was the Schooner Inne.

Mr. Shevvington closed the huge green front doors behind her. It took all his weight to push them shut against the wind. The wind screamed in anger, trying every crack in the house, finding some. The house whistled and shrieked like a demented orchestra. Candle Cove lashed its waves into the cliffs, which threw them back in a chorus of crashes.

She was locked in the sea captain's mansion, alone with crazy Anya, the Shevvingtons, and the poster of the sea.

Chapter 14

The house was completely silent.

Christina looked into Michael and Benj's room before she entered her own. How terrifying empty beds were. The neatness of the sheets and blankets was like the neatness of a mowed and trimmed graveyard.

Anya lay alone in her room, staring at the poster of the sea. The poster shimmered in the dusty dark of early evening, neon tremors of life struggling to be free. "Anya, at least turn on the lights," said Christina.

"You can't see the poster smile except in the dark," explained Anya.

Christina's hair lifted on her head. She could actually feel the colors of her own hair: brown, silver, and gold, trembling for Anya.

"I can't leave the room, either. The poster will come back off the wall again. I'll drown in a paper sea."

Christina backed into the hall, hands feeling the walls, stretching for the banisters of the balcony.

She's already drowned. She drowned inside her mind.

Behind her the house lay quiet, dark, and expectant.

Christina turned to face the house, and the house seemed to whirl behind her, laughing. She turned again, and again, spinning dizzily at the top of the stairs, trying to keep safe, as though something might attack her from behind.

She ran into her room, the house closing at her ankles, catching at her hair, and she dived, fully clothed, into her bed.

Under the covers, under her mother's quilt, she wept till she could weep no more, for Anya and for herself — unloved and alone. Out in Candle Cove the tide began to hum. *Ffffffffff.*

The wind rose and cried out, and the house seemed to talk back, so they were screaming at each other, as if the house and the sea had different plans for the dark of night. *Tonight, Christina, tonight!* they both said.

There were nights when the dark seemed to be her friend, keeping her company through the night — Christina and The Dark — but now the dark was her enemy, keeping her prisoner.

She could feel the evil in the house gathering its forces. Alone she was weaker. She had been separated from her allies, from Michael and Benj and Jonah and Blake — like a gazelle cut from the herd by the lions who would destroy it.

She could not get warm. The bed was piled with

blankets and still the cold got under the covers with her and entered her bones.

Chrissie! Chrissie!

It was the tide calling.

It was the poster of the sea beckoning to her.

Christina whimpered under the covers. Then she remembered that she was granite, not a tern. That Mr. Shevvington did not have the eyes of a mad dog, but of a man who wore contact lenses.

Christina slid out of bed. She wrapped her mother's quilt around herself like a huge calico cape. Within the hood of the quilt she felt protected by her mother's love.

Christina stepped into the hall.

Christina's head and ears filled and pulsed with the huffing. It whirled around her like fans in summer. Humming like bees. *Chrissie, said the house, Chrissie, Chrissie.*

Her eyes and spine burned with fear. Anya was right. The house truly spoke. The sea kept count. It was demanding Christina herself.

A weapon, thought Christina. I need something to hit it with.

She would smother it in the quilt.

Christina walked forward, holding her quilt out like butterfly wings to wrap it in.

She walked into Anya's room. It was wet in there.

The sea is already in here! thought Christina, fear closing over her eyes like lashes. She heard the sea speak her name.

"Chrissie," moaned Anya, "Chrissie, something is wrong. Chrissie, I'm afraid of the poster."

The window was open. Anya was dampened by the rain coming in like cotton waiting to be ironed. The sea said nothing but its usual crash of wave and rock. It was Anya speaking her name.

Christina yanked the sash down, holding the quilt in her teeth so it would not slip off her shoulders.

Then she faced the poster of the sea. Its terrible fingers, its dim, drowning figures, stared back at her.

"I'm in charge here," she said to it. She kept her eyes fastened on the poster. She felt around in Anya's desk and came up with a handful of tacks. She swung the quilt off her shoulders and held it up as if to a charging bull. She rushed the poster.

Outside the wind screamed and the tide rose and Candle Cove fought a war with the rocks and the waves.

Christina covered the poster with the quilt. She tacked the quilt firmly right into the wall. The poster was gone. Calico squares and triangles and tiny firm stitches covered it.

"So there," said Christina.

Anya looked stunned.

"Come on, Anya, let's go downstairs. It isn't healthy up here." Christina dragged Anya out of the bedroom. They marched down to the kitchen, where Christina had her book bag. Anya sat in front of a TV she did not remember to turn on.

Christina tried to read.

From the school library Christina had checked

out a murder mystery Vicki and Gretch had been talking about. At the time she had thought she could read her way into the friendship. It seemed unlikely now. She held the book with her left hand and set the table with her right. Almost before there was a murder, she had figured out who the murderer was. How annoying to be able to add up the clues as easily as third-grade arithmetic.

Mrs. Shevvington had made eggplant lasagne.

"But — but my mother sent baked beans," Christina said.

"You should have refrigerated it," Mrs. Shevvington said. "I had to throw it out. It was no good."

All that love stirred into the molasses, to stick to her ribs like a hug on the island.

Thrown into the trash.

Christina began to cry.

"Everything you do is wrong," said Mrs. Shevvington. She put her hands on her hips, and her weight seemed to double. She rocked back and forth as if planning to topple onto Christina and crush her. "Take that silly baseball cap off."

I need padding, thought Christina. I should wear a soccer goalie's outfit around the house. She found Kleenex and blew her nose and mopped her eyes. Mrs. Shevvington caught the bill of the cap but Christina was ready for her. She whisked the cap behind her back, clutching it with white-knuckled fingers. It may be an anchor, Frankie, Christina thought, but what good is an anchor without a safe harbor?

There is nobody, she thought. I am a ship at sea

without a crew, without a harbor. Nobody loves me. Not Anya, who is hardly even in the room because she hardly even exists. Not Michael or Benj — they never paid enough attention to see anything. Jonah and Blake aren't here. My parents. . . Oh! my parents!

She knew she could never eat the eggplant. She wondered now if she could ever eat again. She felt cleaned out, like a scoured pot. There isn't much left of me right now either, thought Christina.

"Christina, honey," said Mr. Shevvington. He drew her close. He cared. His touch was loving, his embrace warm. Christina leaned on him, absorbing his kindness like a drug. Nothing else could evaporate loneliness. The texture of his jacket made her think of Blake and true love.

"Poor Chrissie," he murmured. "It's been a hard autumn, hasn't it? A girl has daydreams about junior high, and none of them come true, and it's hard to keep going, isn't it?"

Christina nodded, sniffling. The silky tie touched her cheek like a cool finger soothing a fever.

"Tell me all about it," said Mr. Shevvington. His hand closed over hers, warm and comforting.

How she wanted to blame her fears and failures on Mrs. Shevvington, or the seventh grade, or even Anya.

"What are you afraid of, Christina?" he said. "I'm here to help. I know you feel I've been against you, but it's not true, Chrissie. You have me on your team, honey."

His eyes welcomed her home, saying *you'll be safe now. Come to me.*

Very softly, he whispered, "Tell me your fears."

She had so many. They multiplied every day.

Being alone.

Having no friends.

The tide and the wet suit and the glass in the cupola.

The sea captain's bride and the honeymooners and the boy on the bike.

Anya going crazy, Blake gone forever.

How safe were his fatherly arms. His blue eyes were like robins' eggs in a nest, cozy in the tree.

"Tell me about Miss Schuyler," whispered Mr. Shevvington. He patted her hair, dividing the strands into their three colors, and braiding them as her father used to do. "Is Miss Schuyler really tutoring you in arithmetic?" His fingers folded around the baseball cap. His eyes were as soft as a baby blanket.

Perhaps he had looked into Anya's eyes like that, and Val's.

"I have this terrible fear of fractions," Christina told him. She put the baseball cap safely behind her back. "Miss Schuyler thinks she can conquer it. Also a fear of running out of popcorn. Nothing could be worse than going to a movie and they don't have any popcorn, you know?"

"This is not a joke, Christina," said Mr. Shevvington. His grip tightened. His fingers were half white, half tan. "I am trying to be kind, but I expect cooperation from you."

Christina said, "I know about the girls before Val."

The room turned utterly silent.

Mrs. Shevvington stood motionless at the stove. Mr. Shevvington's eyes lay like stones in his head. Beneath the veneer of his blue contact lenses she could see his real eyes. They were not blue. They were ice in winter, gray and cruel.

The Shevvingtons pivoted. Slowly. They faced her. Their eyes drilled into her skull.

"All about them," lied Christina. "All the ones before Val."

She thought of her ancestors who had drowned at sea, and she knew now how they felt: how they saw the power of the wave and the density of the water and knew that their end had come; that their ships were only pitiful bits of kindling in a great and powerful sea.

She had made a mistake. She had gone to sea in a storm. The Shevvingtons would destroy her now as easily as the Atlantic destroyed a sandcastle.

But they did not move toward her. They did not squash her between them. They did not discuss the girls before Val. Instead their horrible eyes met above her head, and their little mouths smiled secretly, and she knew that they had plans she knew nothing of.

Outside, the storm quickened and raged.

All Maine went behind doors and shutters, hunkering down; there was nobody to hear a scream for help, nobody who would be looking out any windows.

They sat down to eggplant. Her mother's casserole dish was on the sink. Scoured clean. Anya ate nothing. Christina ate only a roll. Nobody talked. A meal without conversation is an efficient thing. It was over in moments.

After supper Christina watched television. There was nothing on. This seemed unfair. On the island they hardly got TV at all, mostly watching rented movies on the VCR, and now when she needed electronic company and canned laughter, there was nothing on.

Anya drifted upstairs alone.

She'll be safe, thought Christina. I've locked the window and covered the poster. Sleep is what she needs anyhow.

She wrapped herself in an afghan. The Shevvingtons' eyes followed her every move.

She read her mystery, bored because she already knew the ending, and afraid because the pages were littered with bodies in car trunks, bodies in alleys. With every page turn, the Shevvingtons' eyes grew colder and the afghan protected her less.

But eventually they had to move. Mrs. Shevvington went to her room, Mr. Shevvington to the library.

She was momentarily alone. The rooms of black and gold creaked. Outside the wind lifted even more. She could hear metallic crashes as somebody's garbage can was tossed down Breakneck Hill.

Christina tiptoed from the TV room and into the hall, where she picked up the telephone. She dialed information and then she dialed the number they gave her. Less than one minute and Dexter Academy had connected her to Blake's room. "Blake?" she whispered.

"Hello?" said Blake.

Christina burst into tears.

"Anya?" said Blake. "Is that you?"

Christina shook her head.

"I love you," said Blake. "It'll be all right. I'll think of something. I haven't yet, but I will."

I love you.

"It's me. Christina. Blake, I'm alone with them."

"Chrissie, don't cry." His voice was rich with concern. "Tell me what's happening. How is Anya?"

"Leaning on the washers and dryers soaking up the lint."

"I don't understand why she gave up," said Blake. "Why didn't she keep fighting?"

"She thinks the enemy is her, not them." Christina could not bear to talk about Anya. She had to know whether Blake blamed her the way his parents did. "You don't think I tempted you to die, do you?" *You love me too, don't you, Blake?*

"Of course I don't. I was trying to see who was in the wet suit. I've lived here for years, I know better than to go down a ladder into Candle Cove, I was just being stupid. My parents refuse to believe they raised a stupid son so they're blaming it on you. Chrissie, I've thought and thought about it, and I think the man in the wet suit has a place to go. Under the cliff. Maybe even under Schooner Inne! Maybe that's why the sea talks so loud inside the house. Maybe there's actually a sea passage into the cellar!"

Christina found that almost more horrifying than Anya's belief that the wet suit *was* the sea. But I've never been in the cellar, she thought. I've never even thought about the cellar.

Was the cellar full of water now — full of storm and tide, crawling up the walls of Schooner Inne to drown her in bed?

Christina tried not to cry. She wanted more than anything just to keep listening to Blake's voice. His wonderful, rich, boy's voice. She told Blake about trying to find the fear files and getting caught like a cheap thief. "You don't think I'd steal money, do you?" she said anxiously.

"No, but you might do something else equally dumb. Leave it, Christina, just leave it. They're bigger than you are. More powerful. The Shevvingtons had one talk with my parents — *one!* — and wham! I'm two hundred miles west. I try to tell them it was important to go down the cliff after that man in the wet suit and they tell me not to make things up and how much I'll like boarding school."

She could see him, all lean and handsome and windblown. I love you, she thought. It's wrong and I'm going to stop tomorrow. She said, "We might get a hurricane."

Even as she spoke she heard something come off the house — a shutter or a storm door perhaps —

and rip agonizingly, and crash around in the alley.

"Take care of yourself, Chrissie," he said. There was a catch in his voice. She treasured it. "Listen," she began.

A thick, gnarled finger with chipped layers of red polish disconnected the phone.

"Christina," said Mrs. Shevvington softly, "I have told you not to use the telephone without permission. Who were you calling? We will find out when the bill comes, of course, so do not fib."

Christina did not fib. She did not speak at all.

"Bedtime," said Mrs. Shevvington.

Christina walked up alone, into the waiting dark.

The Shevvingtons stood below on their balcony, their arms folded like chains, and smiled at each other.

She would never sleep. The winds outside were trying to throw the house into Candle Cove. Perhaps the passage in the cellar was undermining the house so it would cave in from the bottom as well.

Every hundred years, thought Christina, turning Frankie's remarks over in her mind. I could read old newspapers, couldn't I? And find out about the boy on the bike and the honeymooners and the sea captain, and even the weather and the tides.

She tugged her hair into a ponytail and stuffed it up under the baseball cap. She had a lot of hair. It made a puffy pillow on top of her head.

On the very last page of the mystery book she found out who the murderer was. She had misunderstood every hint. She had never realized at all who the bad guy was. Christina had been completely tricked.

Had she misunderstood every clue in Schooner Inne as well?

She got out of bed and padded silently into Anya's room, making no noise to disturb her. Standing in the dormer, Christina looked out at Candle Cove. The waves did not curl in pretty frothy fingers. Tons of black and green water sloshed to the cliff tops and fell back. Wind cut canyons through the water. Even as she watched, a dinghy and a small motorboat filled with water and sank. A larger boat tore loose from its mooring and was dashed against its neighbor, hitting it like a sledge, until they both splintered.

The tall utility poles along the parking lot above the wharf threw a thick, mustard-yellow light over the chaos.

There was only one human being visible. Not a fisherman struggling to save his boat nor a house owner trying to fasten a shutter.

Anya.

White as a bride, clinging to the Singing Bridge.

So many clues! thought Christina. I missed every one. *Anya* was cut away from the safety of the rest of us — not me. *Anya* is the endangered species — not me!

Robbie had said that whenever somebody drowned, the bridge sang. Over the fierceness of the storm Christina could not tell if the bridge was singing. She could not call to Anya to stop her.

Tonight, the tide had whispered.

But it had been Anya whispering.

Anya announcing her plans.

Christina ran down the stairs. She had to get to Anya. Fast.

The front door, of course, was locked.

Christina clung to the big brass handle, unable to think at all. How had Anya gotten out? How was Christina to get out?

She raced back up the stairs and pounded on the Shevvingtons' bedroom door. (Did people like that sleep? Or just lie awake, gloating and planning?) "Open up!" she screamed. "We have to go save Anya. Unlock the front door. Get ropes. Call the fire department!"

The Shevvingtons did not open the door.

She shook it hard and kicked it. "I need you!" she screamed. "Help me get Anya."

"Christina, Anya is sound asleep. Go back to bed. This house has withstood a century and a half of storms, and it won't give way to this one."

Christina beat on the door with her fists. "Anya is on the Singing Bridge. She's going to step off into the Cove."

Mr. Shevvington ripped the bedroom door open. He wore a long, dark maroon robe, like Christmas kings. "Stop this!" he roared, louder even than the sea. "Go to bed."

"Look out the window!" cried Christina. She was sobbing now and it was hard to get a deep breath. What if Anya had already gone to the sea?

"We have had enough of your nonsense," said Mr. Shevvington.

She stared at him. "But Anya — "

"Is fine."

"Is going to drown!" she screamed, as if volume could convince, screaming so loudly she was raw in her throat just from those four words.

Mr. Shevvington folded his arms. He stood in the bedroom door staring down at Christina. It seemed to her that the corners of his mouth wanted to smile. Mrs. Shevvington, sitting up in the bed, did smile. Then she pushed the remote control button for her television.

Christina whirled and ran down the stairs to the kitchen. From her book bag she ripped her house key and flew back through the black-and-gold halls to the front door. She jabbed her key in the lock.

It did not fit.

"Your key fits only from the outside, Christina." How mocking was Mrs. Shevvington's voice. How sure of victory!

But victory would be Anya's plunge into Candle Cove. Anya, who thought the sea was keeping count . . . when all along it was the Shevvingtons.

Christina ran to the windows in the living room. Shuttered on the outside against the storm. She ran into the dining room. Shuttered and barred. The kitchen door was locked; the side door locked.

"Stop this!" she screamed. "Let me out! If you won't save Anya, let me!"

Behind their door, the Shevvingtons laughed.

She had thought that in the end they would be Good. That when push came to shove, they were grown-ups; they might be mean, but they would not stand by and let Anya walk off the cliff.

She had been wrong.

She did not live with people who knew the meaning of Good.

Trembling on the stairs, Christina tried to think. She cast her eyes up for some other kind of help. The glass in the cupola winked.

I can get out the top, thought Christina; they haven't closed the bottle entirely.

How long the ladder was. How many rungs there were. As if she were passing into another world, another time.

Christina pushed open the window through which Anya had talked to the sea. She slid out. There on the top of the house — so high it felt like the top of Maine — she stood, a tiny girl on a tiny ledge above the entire Atlantic Ocean.

The gale had gathered the sea and all its creatures and was hurling it mercilessly against the cliffs, reaching for the house. She stood on the roof like a twig in a blender.

I'm here, she thought, but how do I get down? Anya is still on the Singing Bridge, but she can't hear me over the storm!

"Blake!" whispered Christina. She did not have a real voice anymore. She spoke only with the ghost of her lungs. "Somebody — Mother — Daddy — Miss Schuyler — come get me, please!"

She yanked Frankie's baseball cap down hard on her forehead to keep it from blowing away.

Nobody will come get me, Christina thought.

And if anybody is going to get Anya, it has to be me.

Behind her, the window closed. A tiny sound, audible because it was not part of the storm, told Christina the truth. The Shevvingtons had latched the window.

Christina turned, terrified, and lost her balance, slipping backward toward the sea, her bare feet sliding on the cruel roof.

In the cove the waves clapped.

Chapter 15

There was a blur of stars and rain.

There was time to think of the outrage of it all: that she should tumble to her death like the sea captain's bride when she was the *good* one! The Shevvingtons, who deserved a watery grave, would live on.

There was time to think of the horror of her very own lungs filling with water instead of air. Would it hurt? Or would she merely cease to be?

She slanted between the sea and the sky, pummeled with rain, assaulted with noise. Her toes curled on the shingles, trying to hang on. Below her, the sea screamed and taunted. It tossed feathers of sea foam on her bare legs.

She screamed, throwing her hands out, tilting herself backward, trying to lie down, trying —

But there was nothing there.

Her feet reached into space, gravity yanked her body after them, and her hands held only air.

Christina landed immediately. Even her feet were surprised, and both her ankles turned in, having assumed, in a muscle and bone way, that they would never again hold up her body. She was standing on the sill formed by the odd little dormer of Anya's bedroom.

Her tears of terror blended with the rain, as if she were one with the clouds.

Below her the roof formed a very slanted passage away from the sea cliffs, toward the street. She crawled onto the shingles, trying not to think of the waiting arms of the waves below. The roof sloped more steeply than Breakneck Hill. There had to be a window she could get in. She caught the edge of a shutter and clung to it, trying to get away from the sea. It was the window of the Shevvingtons' bedroom. She could see their shadows.

She thought of the sea captain's bride. Had she tried to catch herself, too? She thought of Anya. Was this Anya's route — or had the Shevvingtons let her out, knowing Anya's state of mind?

Christina crawled forward, slithering closer and closer to the grim edge. The rain caught on the shingles and glittered like diamonds that would never be strung on necklaces. Don't slow down, she told herself. If you stop to think about what you're doing, you'll panic.

Below her was the nearly flat roof of the kitchen stoop. Christina inched down the wet shingles, clung for a moment to the gutters, dangled her feet as far as she could, and let go.

She could not even hear the thud of her own feet landing. The sound of the storm had drowned the sound of her crash.

Anya, wait for me! Christina thought. Her chest hurt from the desperate thudding of her own heart.

One more jump to go. Down into the back alley. But this last jump would be the worst; pavement was hard, unforgiving. The ocean might call, *Float in me*. The earth made no such promises. *Break your bones on me*, said the earth.

She jumped, landing knees first in a puddle full of sodden leaves. Her knees were skinned and bleeding. Her insides felt jarred loose. She stared up at Schooner Inne. She could not believe the height she had come down. She saw the Shevvingtons rushing from window to window, trying to figure out where Christina was now.

"I got down," she whispered. "I'm off the roof, Anya. I'm coming, just wait for me." Her knees buckled and left her in the puddle. She had to crawl. Like a whipped puppy she pulled herself forward, crying uselessly into the wind. "Anya, Anya, don't do anything!"

Every light in Schooner Inne went on.

It's not enough they won't help, Christina thought, they're going to come out and stop me! Oh, I hate them! How I hate them!

Christina hauled herself up, ran out the alley, and down the black steepness of Breakneck Hill.

How fast I'm going! she thought. I've never run so fast in my life.

It was like flying. She did not even seem to be using her feet. She was windblown, like a seabird in the air currents.

This is how the boy on his bike felt, she thought.

It was worth it to him. He was happy when he —

When he broke his neck.

Christina grabbed the fence, tearing her fingers on the thin, harsh metal. She slowed herself with her hands, braking with her palms.

Then she forced herself to walk. She counted her steps, making her feet land hard and flat. One hand was bleeding. She wrapped it in —

Oh, no, thought Christina. I'm wearing my nightshirt.

It was an XXXL barn-red T-shirt on which her mother had embroidered Christina's name in silver thread.

I look like a Christmas card. If they see me wearing a T-shirt and absolutely nothing else on a cold Maine October night, they'll lock me up. I'll be Val's roommate.

Singing Bridge was empty, no cars hummed over its metal treads.

She was too late. Anya had gone to the sea.

Sobbing, Christina rushed to the edge of the cliffs.

Candle Cove, too, looked like a Christmas card. Waves curled in shepherd's crooks, layers of white sea foam icing on green cakes. There, climbing down to the ledge where the honeymooners had picnicked, was Anya, clad all in white.

Anya glanced up and waved as sweetly as if they were at a school soccer game, cheering goals. "I heard you call," said Anya, happily, who could not have heard anything above the roar of the elements. "I heard you say to wait for you. I'm so glad we're going together, Christina." Anya's face was invisible, clouded by the black hair that frothed in the wind, glittering with diamonds of night mist.

Christina knelt by the terrible wet cliffs, and the shepherd's crooks of water tried to hook her body and drag her into the final fold. I have already climbed down a house! thought Christina. I can't face these rocks. I can't fight the sea again.

Anya took Christina's hand, light as air, and pulled her down. Over a sea-slippery ledge they went, and down to the next one, the waves crashing over their knees.

"No, Anya," Christina cried. "I figured something out. One evil attracts another. Each terrible thing makes space for another terrible thing. Terrible things and terrible people warm to each other. But we can defeat the Shevvingtons. I know we can, Anya. Stop going toward the sea, Anya."

Anya smiled. "We'll go together, Chrissie. They did that a lot in the olden days, you know."

"Did what?"

"Went back to the sea." Anya turned her face up to the storm.

"We didn't come from the sea," Christina pointed out. "We came from the island."

Anya shook her head. "We're not going that far." She pulled Christina with her.

The wind blew Frankie's cap off Christina's head and tossed it skywards. It spun in circles like a maddened scarlet bird and flew through the sky toward land. Christina screamed, and tried to reach it, but it was no use.

Anya nodded. "There is no magic stronger than the sea," she said to Christina. Anya had far more strength than Christina did. No matter how hard Christina pulled at her to go back up, Anya could pull harder to go down. This seemed odd to Christina, since it was Anya who was the tern.

If I were granite, thought Christina, I would be heavy enough to hold her.

She had nothing: no talisman, no quilt, no cap, no arguments.

And no strength.

She was sapped.

"Blake needs you," Christina told Anya. Even as she spoke, she thought, If only Blake could need *me*! Even as the water covered her thighs and the terrible steps they were taking were hidden beneath the waves, she saw his catalog Maine clothes and his windblown hair, and heard his warm voice, and wished that just once more, she could have his hand over hers. But Blake does need me, she thought. To save Anya.

Sea foam spun over them. Anya caught it in her hands, like lace to be measured for a wedding gown.

"Blake loves you!" Christina cried. "I don't have the quilt and I don't have the cap and I don't have the strength of granite, but I still have love. Come on, Anya, we're leaving the sea behind. It won't take us. Now or ever. It has all the dead it needs." She gripped Anya's hand with both of hers and lunged into the wind.

Anya fought.

The sea curled around Christina's bare feet. The

seaweed clinging to the rocks was brown slick. The barnacles tore her flesh.

"Anya, we have to go back up," shrieked Christina. "We'll die here! We don't want to die, we don't even want to catch cold!"

"Die?" said Anya, surprised.

"What did you think would happen under water?"

"I am of the sea."

"So am I, but mostly I'm of the island. Climb, Anya, climb!"

Christina looked back at Anya to smile at her, give her courage, but she saw only what Blake had seen: a wall of black water coming to get her. The sea was a mathematician. The sea kept count. They were the island princesses, marked out for sacrifice.

"Well, I'm not coming!" Christina Romney screamed. The wave hit her as hard as a boxer, filling her face and mouth with sea water. She spat it out. Gripping Anya, dragging her up, Christina stretched for the torn metal fence. She needed another hand; she could not hold onto Anya, and to the rocks, and to her own life, all at the same time.

The next wave knocked them back, down toward the honeymooner's ledge. Amidst the colors of darkness and storm she seemed to see a glitter of gold and silver, as if the ribbons from Dolly's package still danced on the waves.

My hair. Silver and gold.

Anya was right after all: the sea did follow me. It does want me.

Christina sobbed. Her fingers lost their tenuous

grip. Anya, who had never tried anyway, slid feet-first into the waves.

Christina tried to shout at Anya, but her mouth filled with salt water.

"It's no use," said Anya, saying good-bye to the world.

"It is so!" said Christina. "Now I'm mad. Now I've had enough. Get up, Anya Rothrock! Don't you fade into that water like some dumb honeymooner. Don't you slip down like some stupid kid on a bike. Get up, Anya Rothrock!"

Rage propelled Christina forward, up over the rocks, up over the fence, into the sodden street.

The only place in town that was open all night was the laundromat.

It was warm in there.

In a lifetime of swimming, diving, and boats, Christina had never been so wet. She was wet from her skin to her bone marrow. Her tri-colored hair ran like a river. She shuddered over and over, remembering the roofs and the rocks. Where did I get the strength to do that? she thought.

In the black glass of the laundromat door she saw her reflection: a small child. A seventh-grader. Nobody impressive.

Anya held out her hands to the warmth of the tumbling dryers and whispered, "Did we win, Chrissie? Did we defeat the sea?"

Where evil is, it multiplies, Christina thought. But goodness also multiplies.

"It wasn't the sea that was the enemy," said Christina. "The sea is just there, Anya. It never changes." Christina rummaged among the neat, still toasty-warm stacks of folded clothing Anya had left behind. She pulled on a pair of Anya's jeans, turning up the cuffs several times to shorten them.

The fogged-up door of the laundromat opened.

The Shevvingtons stood there. They were wearing yellow mackinaws. They dripped their own ocean of water onto the floor.

Anya was toweling her hair dry. She looked up vaguely. "Oh, hi there," said Anya, sounding sane, although rather forgetful. "Isn't it awful out?"

The Shevvingtons aren't actually murderers, Christina thought. They spill no blood, stop no hearts. Instead they cut away pride, they cut away purpose. So Val's body, or Anya's body, goes on — while the girl inside flickers and goes out.

Candle Cove.

I thought "candle" referred to the tide and the sea.

Perhaps it means the people who live by the edge: fragile flames struggling not to be blown out.

But I am not fragile. I was not blown out.

I saved Anya. Look at her, worrying about her hair like a normal person.

Christina had a tremendous sense of her power. Like granite she was: stone and rock. Her small body did not seem like something from the seventh grade. More like something cut from the quarries of the islands of Maine.

Christina drew herself up. She flaunted her

power before the Shevvingtons. They seemed to nod, almost to bow, their yellow mackinaws bending in the middle, as if they had become her puppets. Now she, Christina, would pull the strings.

"Is your car here?" said Christina to the Shevvingtons. She was almost laughing. The principal and the teacher were nothing. Tall, yes. In charge, no. "Pull it up in front," ordered Christina. "Take us home. When we get there fix us something hot to eat. Make hot chocolate for Anya."

She was obeyed.

They did not argue with her.

I have won, Christina Romney exulted. She tossed her silver-and-gold hair like banners of triumph, and she swaggered out of the laundromat, leading Anya by the hand.

She was only a seventh-grader. She knew nothing. She did not know that people do not surrender power so easily. She forgot the secret plans she had seen them make over her head during supper.

She did not see how docile Anya was. That toweling her hair dry was the most that Anya could achieve; that Anya took Christina's hand because Anya did not know where to go on her own. That Anya was alive . . . but emptied.

Christina thought she had won.

Chapter 16

It was a wonderful week in school.

There were no appointments with Miss Frisch. There was not a Miss Frisch at all as far as Christina saw.

In English class Mrs. Shevvington did not read Christina's paper out loud to sneer. The Friday essay was ordinary: Hallowe'en costumes they'd worn when they were little.

Vicki and Gretch were still popular and still ignored Christina, but another girl named Jennie, whom Christina had not noticed before, sat with her at lunch. Jennie was loads of fun — perky and silly. Soon they were joined by Kathleen, and then somehow Jonah and Robbie got the courage to sit there, too. They were the first in the seventh grade to have boys and girls at the same table. The rest were envious; even Gretch and Vicki were envious.

Jonah said he'd forgive Christina for refusing to go with him to the Getting To Know You Dance, as long as she promised to come to the Hallowe'en

Party at the Y with him. Christina allowed Jonah to hold her hand for just a moment. Hand-holding looked glorious when seniors did it, but it was pretty icky for seventh-graders.

Kathleen and Jennie giggled, ducking their heads and blushing and making incredibly dumb remarks.

Christina said she would dress up as an island princess for the Hallowe'en Party: what would Jonah be?

Jonah said since Christina thought he had a graveyard name, he was going to be his own tombstone.

Vicki and Gretch said loftily that seventh-graders were too old for that kind of silliness.

Three more kids, who felt being silly was much more fun than hanging around with Vicki and Gretch, moved over to Christina's table. Hers was now the most crowded. People offered her their desserts. They spoke wistfully of her hair, wishing theirs was three-colored, too. They even asked where she got her jeans.

I wouldn't be surprised if I can do anything, Christina thought. I will be able to get Anya back in high school. Blake will telephone me. Next time Michael and Benj go home for the weekend, I'll go, too. Mother and Daddy will love me again. I will get proof for Miss Schuyler and we'll get rid of the Shevvingtons for once and for all.

It was too bad that Miss Schuyler was sick all that glorious week and they had a substitute teacher for arithmetic. Christina wanted to tell Miss Schuyler everything.

Monday I'll tell her, thought Christina. She'll be proud of me.

Christina sauntered home from school.

The sky had cleaned itself up, swept itself clear.

There was something terrible, almost insane, the way there was never any trace of the weather in the sky.

Earth and sea carried debris. Broken tree limbs, downed wires, sunken ships.

But the sky was fresh and new, no ripples, no scars in its deep indigo blue.

The air was a symphony of rustles and shivers: distant wings of migrating flocks, softly slapping waves, the humming of the Singing Bridge.

Even the Shevvingtons realize, thought Christina, gloating, hot with pride, this time they tangled with somebody they cannot frighten. I can walk down roofs during gales. I can save people from drowning. What is a mere school principal to me?

She swaggered a little, although it was difficult on the slant of Breakneck Hill.

Mrs. Shevvington had gotten back to Schooner Inne before Christina.

Mr. Shevvington, strangely enough, was also home early.

Together they opened the great green doors, and, together, smiling, they welcomed Christina home. Because I'm in charge and they know it, thought Christina.

She walked in between them.

Behind her they closed the great green doors and turned the lock.

Christina merely shrugged and carried her book bag up to her room. She had bought her own snack today; it didn't matter whether the Shevvingtons thought there was too much sugar in it or not.

She ran up the stairs, just to show them they couldn't dictate anything to her, including the speed of using the stairs.

In her dark green room, her mother's quilt lay soft on her bed.

Fffffffffffff, said the house.

Christina stood very still in the hall. She turned very slowly. She walked around the balcony. The boys' room was the same as ever, Marilyn Monroe smiling down from the wall. But in Anya's room, the empty second bed was now made. Suitcases sat unopened on the floor by the second bed. Another chest of drawers had been set by the dormer window.

Her mother's quilt had been taken down.

The poster of the sea was exposed.

No, thought Christina.

The room stank of low tide, of clams and mussels and dead things. Christina reached for the wall but it slid away, like a fish under water. *Ffffff* said the walls and the floor and the glass. She tried to stand up, but there was weight on her, as if she were standing under water, with a million tons of green ocean pressing down.

It can't happen again! she thought. The poster

is only a poster. The sea is only water.

She licked her lips and they tasted of salt.

It's Candle Cove, it's the tide, she reminded herself. The house is just a house. I identified the evil, and it's the Shevvingtons.

She grabbed the banister.

She could not remember the way downstairs. She smelled the sweat of the sea. Clinging to the rail, she swam down the stairs.

"Christina," said Mrs. Shevvington. She was laughing. The laugh rattled, like dried peas in a half empty jar.

Christina turned the corner of the stair where the carpet began. She could see the Shevvingtons now. The surf inside her head ceased. Whose suitcases are those? she thought, confused. Not Anya's.

Mrs. Shevvington's little corn teeth matched her laugh. "We have a surprise for you, Christina," she giggled. The giggle was hideous and out of season, like Christmas tree bulbs in July.

Why did the room seem colder? What draft curled around Christina's heart?

Christina reached the hall. Mr. Shevvington stood on her right, Mrs. Shevvington on her left.

"You're lonely," said Mrs. Shevvington. "You need the companionship of another girl. One closer to your age than Anya, Christina."

"Of course, a principal has a certain amount of discretion," said Mr. Shevvington. "Rules of school attendance can be altered for special situations. The rule is, Christina, that a child goes to school on the island until seventh grade. But we petitioned to have that changed, Christina. Your parents are so happy, Christina; they feel you're going to be calmer now that you have a friend."

"I have plenty of friends," Christina said.

There was a patter of feet from the kitchen.

The Shevvingtons turned, laughing, to see who came.

It was Dolly.

Sweet.

Innocent.

Another Val. Another Anya.

How Dolly danced, red curls free from braids. Her body was elementary school size; a fragile collection of bones in bib overalls. "Isn't it wonderful?" she cried to Christina. "Can you believe my luck? I'm off-island, too!" She turned her pixie smile into the towering faces of the Shevvingtons. "I get to attend sixth grade here!" She took the Shevvingtons' hands and swung their heavy arms back and forth like a set from a square dance. "The Shevvingtons have been so wonderful to me, Chrissie," she said. "I'm going to love living here!" She hardly saw Christina. She beamed into their eyes. Mr. Shevvington's eyes were as blue as they had ever been, and, like the sky, they were swept clean of the past.

They were nothing, they were blanks.

On which to compose the storm that would take Dolly Jaye.

Christina's pride dwindled away like a ship vanishing over the horizon. She wet her lips. "I told Miss Schuyler," Christina began.

Mr. Shevvington's smile spread wider and wider, exposing more and more teeth, like a crocodile. "Your little math teacher? I'm afraid she found another job, Christina. Out west somewhere. Such a loss."

Mr. Shevvington put his arm around Christina. It might have been a hug or the beginning of a strangle. "You'll never be able to replace her, Christina. Will you?"

Fffffffff, said the house.

But only Christina seemed to hear.

"Now, Dolly, remember, this is a special privilege," said Mr. Shevvington. How caring he looked. How fatherly and kind. How blue his eyes were. "You must try very hard to prove that I am right to bring you among us a year early, Dolly."

"I won't let you down!" cried Dolly eagerly. "I'll do anything you say."

"I know," said the principal.

You'll want to read The Snow,
Book Two in the new Point horror trilogy.

Excerpt from The Snow:

Dolly had the right constitution for reading. She could curl up in the old chair and sit for hours, flicking pages.

Christina sometimes preferred to have movement and space. She wanted to kick and run and swing her arms. Books sometimes slowed her down; she had to be in the mood for a book. Dolly was always in the mood for a book.

Sometimes Dolly thought she was wrong to spend so much time choosing books. Especially after the principal said, "Too much reading, Dolly. I'm suspending your library privileges."

Dolly went to the town library instead.

Mr. Shevvington had her library card taken away.

Dolly had her friends in the sixth grade smuggle her books. But they had no book sense. They checked out junk like *Ronnie and the Little League Mystery*, or *The Story of the Boston Fish Market*.

"I always thought I would make an excellent invalid," said Dolly one night at supper. "I like bed. I like sheets and pillows. I'd lie there and read. All

I need is enough strength to turn pages."

"Perhaps you could have an accident," said the principal softly.

"I would be very brave," Dolly agreed.

The principal smiled.

About the Author

Caroline Cooney lives in a small seacoast village in Connecticut, with three children and two pianos. She writes every day on a word processor and then goes for a long walk down the beach to figure out what she's going to write the following day. She's written about thirty-five books for young people, but THE FOG, THE SNOW, and THE FIRE is her first horror series. She also plays the piano for the school music programs, is learning jazz, reads a mystery novel a night, and does a lot of embroidery.